Is Your Child Safe At School?

Is Your Child Safe At School?

Basil Scion

Edited by Jodey Edwards-Kelly

Table of Contents

Chapter One   Betrayal   1
Chapter Two   First Rehearsal   15
Chapter Three   Teaching Respect   23
Chapter Four   Dress Rehearsal   37
Chapter Five   Spite   52
Chapter Six   Left Out in the Cold   74
Chapter Seven   Work Day   103
Chapter Eight   Celebration   150
Chapter Nine   Vigil   172

Basil Scion Biography   175

Betrayal

A stranger's car was parked in the driveway. Coming back from a workshop early, Dwaine Mann could only think of one explanation for the unknown car. With a feeling of nausea, he slowly unlocked the front door and walked into the house.

He had been told by Bea Ogletree, a neighbor, that Gayle had been seeing a man during his deployment. Gayle was the love of his life, and Dwaine had never cheated on her. Despite what his neighbor had said, he knew that she would always be faithful. Bea had told him that Gayle had gone to a divorce attorney, and Dwaine had dismissed it as the gossip of a jealous old woman.

As he walked in, he swore to himself that he was hearing things. There were moaning sounds coming from the back bedroom. "Oh God, don't stop," Gayle said as Dwaine approached. "Don't stop..."

He opened the door and saw his beloved wife on top of some guy he had never seen before. His vision began to blur and before he knew it, he was blacking out. Trying to keep quiet, he grabbed the door to hold on, but it made a slight creak.

Gayle stopped and turned her head around, seeing him.

Kill them. Dwaine heard a distinct, deep, and raspy voice with a savage intent in his head. With a blank stare on his face, the voice directed him. He grabbed for the gun at his side, then held it up and aimed.

Still naked, Gayle stood up and ran away. Her lover reached for his gun on the bedside table.

Stop her. Dwaine reached out to grab Gayle as she ran though the doorway, but he missed and was slapped on his face.

Looking back, Dwaine saw the lover's gun aimed at him.

He couldn't tell who shot first, but Dwaine didn't miss and the lover did.

Gayle, seeing her lover shot, yelled, "You killed him, you son of a bitch!" The words did not register in his mind. She ran to the kitchen.

With a stoic face and gun in hand, Dwaine went after her. She waited for him to come around the refrigerator. When he walked by she attacked him with a serrated knife, stabbing him in the shoulder. The cut added an element of acute pain, the shock of which awoke him from his trance.

He dropped the gun and pushed Gayle back. Now fearing for his life, he said, "Just put the knife down."

"I am pregnant with his child, you idiot. I was about to divorce you," Gayle said, continuing, "You are always gone."

"Just calm down," he pleaded.

She came at him again.

"Gayle, stop. Please stop." She pulled her arm up high, and then brought down the knife to make the kill.

Dwaine caught her hand as it came down. "Gayle, stop," he said.

She relented and dropped the knife. She took a couple steps back, and before he knew it, she had grabbed his gun off the floor and pointed it at him.

Attack her, the voice said in his mind.

Before he could act, a bullet came through the glass pane of the French door and hit Gayle, dropping her to the ground. The police saw through the door that she had pulled the gun on Dwaine.

Dwaine went to his wife to hold her for the last time, a gesture he had too often taken for granted.

"No, sir, don't touch her," the police officer said as he and his partner entered the house.

While clutching his shoulder, Dwaine could only look at her body, and then at the officer. He shook his head.

"Stay where you are, sir," the officer instructed him. Moving forward, Officer Edwards bent over and checked Gayle to make sure she was no longer a threat.

While the officer was bent over, Dwaine looked at Officer Murphy and said, "What the hell have you done?"

"Saved your life, it looks like," the officer said, then continued, "Murphy to Central."

Dwaine saw his gun in Gayle's dead hands.

"Go ahead," a voice spoke from his radio.

"Code 998, send Crime Scene Unit, EMT, and coroner."

"Be advised, there is a 10 – 60."

Officer Murphy turned back to Dwaine. "Another unit is on the way. Is there anyone else in the house, or is it just you and the lady?"

"Look, I don't remember much. All I remember is a guy in the back bedroom pulled a gun on me," Dwaine said, looking the police officer in the eye. He reached in his pocket.

"No sir, keep your hands out where I can see them," Murphy told him.

"I was just going to call an attorney," Dwaine said.

"That can wait," Murphy said as he patted Dwaine down. He found the smart phone and wallet. He quickly took out the id and a gun permit.

Confirming that the house was his residence, he said, "Ok so you live here."

"Yes, sir."

Holding the gun permit, he asked, "Is that your gun?"

"It is mine."

"Are there any more weapons in the house?"

"Like I said the other the guy had a gun in the bedroom. But I don't have any more guns."

Dwaine thought that maybe now was not the time to tell him that he needed to take his medicine.

◆ ◆ ◆

When the other unit arrived, Officer Murphy said to the arriving unit, "House is not secure." Their guns drawn, Officer Murphy led Officer Rogers to check the other rooms. Officer Edwards, a rookie, stayed behind with Dwaine. Working their way back to master bedroom, the police searched every room.

In the master bedroom, they found a man, around mid-twenties, in the bed with a shot to his head.

"Look at this," Officer Rogers said, pointing to the bullet hole in the wall near the door.

They approached cautiously, checking all angles of the room. No danger presented itself.

Murphy turned to Rogers and said, "Here is what it looks like. The man in the kitchen is the husband." He paused, "He walks in on the wife screwing this guy in the master bedroom. He pulls a gun and shoots. But I don't know how she picked up the gun, and I don't know is if this was murder or self-defense."

"Not our call to make. Forensic will need to process the house," Officer Rogers said.

♦ ♦ ♦

The investigating unit arrived and took a statement from Dwaine. He was arrested on suspicion of murder. An attorney came to see him in jail.

"What do you remember, son?" he asked.

"I'll tell you like I told them, I just remember seeing a guy in my bed screwing my wife," Dwaine said.

"The man you saw had a gun. From what I read in the police report, he aimed the gun at you and fired. The prosecutor will not be able to prove who shot first. But the fact is Gayle's lover pulled a gun on you."

He continued, "It's probably best that you blanked out when you did. It indicates a case of extreme emotional trauma. I'll get you out of here on reasonable doubt."

"What do you mean?" Dwaine said.

"The point I am driving at is this was self-defense. Your training kicked in when you saw the gun aimed at you. Anyone would have done the same thing."

Dwaine looked down, shaking his head.

"Hey son, don't look so unhappy. I am getting you off and out of jail."

"You are?" Dwaine asked.

"Yeah, be glad you have some rich relatives, or you would really have a reason to look sad." The attorney chuckled. "There is one more thing. Get used to the phrase 'Justifiable Use of Force.' You will have to mention that when you apply for jobs. What are you planning to do after you leave the service?"

"What else? Teach."

A New Tradition

Mount Reese Academy was located in the growing city of Statesboro, North Carolina, in the eastern portion of Picks County. Due to recent population growth, the academy now accommodated both elementary and middle-school students of all races. The sleepy southern town had once been served by only narrow, two-lane roads. Now it boasted several bustling four-lane highways. Big box stores were dispersed conveniently next to big bookstores and furniture stores. These were surrounded by franchised restaurants and smaller retail stores. Every other nook, cranny, and alley in the town held the odd sprinkling of houses and apartments. New construction had brought a wealth of new families and money into the community. While the rest of the United States lagged in unemployment, Picks County was now one of the top ten fastest growing counties in America, and it was leading growth in the state of North Carolina. Because of the economic boom, Statesboro started to experience the common traffic problems of a metropolitan city.

Beginning five years ago, Picks and surrounding counties had seen a sharp increase in ethnic diversity, and now the streets were populated with citizens from a variety of ethnic backgrounds. Stores throughout Statesboro now celebrated the roots of such citizens via a wealth of foods, clothing, and various items. This year was going to mark a monumental achievement. It would see the first African American Heritage Celebration held at Mount Reese Academy.

Monday morning, transferred Assistant Principal Victoria Lawrence strolled confidently down the hall as if on a mission. She stood barely over five feet, three inches tall, but the intensity radiating from her eyes gave the impression that she was much taller. She never could control her eyebrows. They forced themselves into each other, creating a perpetual scowl. But her mood was lighter than normal that day. She muttered a remark, "Finally, it's time we get the respect we're due." Her lips quivered as she verbalized the thought.

As she turned towards the classrooms, Victoria's thoughts inevitably returned to memories that had resurfaced. *Maybe it will never be over. But respect. We are going to get respect if it kills us.* She had grown up well after the racially tense times of the 1960s, but she knew those times had directly affected her family. Her grandparents had been beaten at a voting rights march in the 1960s by white supremacists and assaulted when they went to the polls to vote in the 1964 presidential election. When Victoria had grown up to a point where she could understand the past, she was told that her grandfather had been gunned down by a white man with a rattlesnake tattoo on his arm. A fear of snakes, especially rattlesnakes, still plagued her from time to time. While the tragic events had happened before her time, she vowed never to forget her history.

Victoria loved teaching and she was a favorite among the students. When her promotion to Assistant Principal had come, she'd enthusiastically accepted the new position. Yet it hadn't taken long for her to realize that everything would not have an easy fix. She was acutely aware of the many struggles that she herself had faced in dealing with teachers and students. She knew there would be issues, one after another.

At Mount Reese Academy, teachers were always coming in late. And many teachers saw parent communications as a waste of time. The academy had allotted too much flexibility in the rules for the staff. A more proactive approach was required. If teachers didn't care, why would students?

Victoria shook her head in disgust. There were times she felt taken advantage of by those who were supposed to be molding the children. However, all those problems were momentarily forgotten as she walked the halls and observed the young children going to class, excitement on their faces. She made an effort to encourage the students, even though cheerleading was slightly outside her comfort zone. She realized that it was important to throw on a broad smile to exemplify a positive attitude.

"This is a big occasion, kids. Do your best and make Mount Reese look good!" Victoria bellowed.

"We will, Ms. Lawrence!" the students shouted back in unison.

She was smiling more than usual. Not only was she beaming with pride over the commencement of Black History Month and the upcoming Black Heritage Celebration at the academy, but her wedding was also coming up in a few days. She was authentically happy.

Victoria turned and saw Mrs. Howard, a social studies teacher. She was down the hallway, walking with determination. Victoria stopped her to catch up on the preparations. "How are the plans going?" Victoria asked.

Victoria felt a tug. She looked down; it was a young boy. "Give me a moment... Jay, is it?" The boy was small for a sixth-grader, but he was very bright and had skipped the fifth grade.

"Please..." Jay said, likely seeing the look of annoyance on Victoria's face.

"One moment," Victoria said curtly. The boy was an emotional wreck, tugging on her arm. But, whatever it was, it could wait.

"Well, umm," Mrs. Howard said hesitantly.

"Well, what?" Victoria asked.

"Some teachers are not... well, they are dragging their feet."

"Who are you talking about? This isn't the time to be dragging feet."

"Well, it is Mr. Mann. He was supposed to create a slideshow presentation." Mrs. Howard looked irritated.

"It figures," Victoria mumbled under her breath. "Have you confronted him about it?"

"Of course I have, on several occasions, but he keeps putting it off—I think on purpose. Others have done their parts, but Mr. Mann was assigned the slideshow. It is vital to the main presentation," Mrs. Howard added.

Victoria felt another tug on her arm. "One minute child!" she said to Jay. "Good morning, Mr. Turner," she said as the other teacher approached. Jay started to squirm in panic and whimper loudly. Victoria looked down at the boy again. "Give me a moment, please."

"Good morning," Mr. Turner said, right before taking Jay's arm and walking away with the boy.

"Let's go find Mr. Mann in a moment and deal with this," Victoria said sternly.

Mr. Mann's irresponsible and unprofessional attitude had annoyed her from the beginning. She didn't believe he was worthy to be called a teacher. She didn't know what his problem was, but she wasn't about to let him ruin such a historic moment for the academy.

Confrontation

Dwaine had come to Mount Reese three years earlier for his first civilian job after serving in the military. He had found adjustment to civilian life difficult. The organization at the academy was shoddy at best, and the lack of discipline was a joke.

Dwaine was deep in thought as he shuffled down the hall. He had heard Ms. Lawrence's earlier comment, "Finally, it's time we get the respect we are due." He had nearly collided with her as they both had turned the hallway corner. The statement hadn't set well with him, and it was causing his mind to race.

He now stood directly in front of Ms. Lawrence as Mrs. Howard stood nearby. Dwaine tensed up, not knowing how to respond. He clenched his fists tight, as if to keep his anger within him. An image from his ancestor's diary, which Dwaine had obtained a number of years earlier, flashed across his mind. *My God, I will never be able to let this go.* He bit his lower lip, wishing he were somewhere else.

He noticed how Ms. Lawrence was standing in front of him, gritting her teeth. He knew she was just as unhappy to see him as he was to see her. She was small in stature, but he was apprehensive about the authority that she had over him. He took in a deep breath. She pivoted slightly on her high heels to meet his eyes with a deep and penetrating gaze. She flipped her shoulder-length dark hair, which he recognized as a sign that she meant business.

"Ms. Lawrence, good to see you today. I was just bringing the special needs modifications for you to sign," he said, while adding in his mind, *You bossy bitch.*

"Mr. Mann, it has come to my attention that you were directed to create a slideshow presentation for the upcoming Black Heritage Celebration."

"Yeah, I was getting around to it. I was trying to find some relevant pictures to include."

"The rehearsal is today, Mr. Mann. When can I expect it to be finished?"

"Well, I guess I will wrap it up today."

"Make it a priority," she snarled at him. Her eyes never left his, and they never blinked. Dwaine thought it was a good thing they had met with kids around, so she wouldn't lose her cool with him... again.

"I have all these other things to do, too."

"Put this at the top of the list," she said.

"You mean over the modifications, the hour-long faculty meetings, and the parents' conferences? There's a lot to get done ahead of a celebration."

She responded with an unflinching stare, her jaw set and lips pursed.

"Speaking of which," he said, "You need to sign the special needs modifications." He tried to conjure up some authority by pointing out her responsibility on the matter. For added emphasis, he tucked the document folder under his arms and crossed them. His right hand slid up his left arm, pushing his short sleeve upward to uncover a tattoo of a flag with a rattlesnake in its center. Under the flag were inked the words: DON'T TREAD ON ME! He'd gotten the tattoo in high school in response to a teacher riding his ass about discipline. He had hoped that Ms. Lawrence would see it and take the hint.

She cringed at the tattoo. It was highly offensive to her, which she had told him the first time she'd seen it. She sidelined the directive, saying slowly and purposefully, "Get the presentation done."

"Well, you still need to sign these modifications." He stood up straighter and leaned in towards her. Victoria simply accepted his challenge by taking a step closer and pointing her finger.

"Take it to the office." She paused and looked directly at his arm, "And cover up that tattoo." She then promptly left.

Students were walking by, and one of them asked, "Mr. Mann, can you bring that ladder to the gym later?"

"You bet, Rashad. I have to go to the gym and help hook things up. Hey, how did you do on that English test you were stressing over?"

"Aw, Mr. Mann, it was terrible. I only made a B+."

"A B+ is nothing to be ashamed of, but I know you'll do better."

"Thanks, Mr. Mann! I'll keep working. I'm not giving up on my dream of becoming an attorney." Rashad put up his fist for a fist bump.

Dwaine took a second to stop what he was doing, shifted the paperwork to his other arm and reciprocated the gesture.

"I'm the Man!" they both said together. Dwaine brought his fist back and spread his fingers wide in a theatrical fashion. Rashad turned a giggle into a smile.

It was students like Rashad that inspired Dwaine and made him want to be the best Business and Information Technology teacher in the state. He owed it to the students to provide the best education possible, and he wanted to set a good example for them. He had made a point to educate himself on all new technology dealing with networks, hardware, software, and the problem of hacking. His students were going to learn everything he was required to teach, but Dwaine also wanted to bring real-life concepts, issues, and problems into the classroom to make learning interesting and meaningful.

Professional Development Plan

A thinning hairline prompted Dwaine to wear a ball cap most of the time. His favorite cap was a gift and was signed by his former unit members. A '2nd' was written in big letters across the top and, in a smaller size, 'Amendment.'

But he knew it was this cap that had started things off on the wrong foot with Ms. Lawrence. From the beginning, she had let him know that she didn't like it. In August of that school year, when Ms. Lawrence first transferred to Mount Reese, she'd gotten in Dwaine's face, reaching for his cap as she said, "No hats in the building."

"What are you doing, lady?" he had shouted at her.

He hadn't known exactly who she was yet, but later she was pointed out by another teacher as one of the administrators. He had worn the cap again the next day out of spite more than anything, daring her to say something again. Although she had maintained her distance that day, he had seen the contempt in her eyes.

Ever since that incident, Ms. Lawrence had regarded Dwaine with vile indignation. The ball cap and a comment about the poor discipline in the academy were going to cause problems for him. Dwaine knew Ms. Lawrence would have a Professional Development Plan for him. Teacher reprimands were different in every state, but in theory, PDPs were meant to help teachers, but in reality they were like crosses to vampires.

A vindictive principal could assign one on a whim. Dwaine remembered Ms. Lawrence's sarcastic comments on the observation sheet. The classroom observation was the tool needed to start a PDP. He had convinced himself that she had written 'Needs Improvement' prior to the actual observation on each the four different sections: content knowledge, standards, classroom environment, and classroom management. *Damn administrators*. He had thought about reporting her, but if nothing happened as a result, he'd have to deal with the consequences. And she would certainly provide him with consequences.

His actual observation had been a farce. The trouble was only three marks of 'Needs Improvement' were allowed on a classroom observation. Thanks to the fourth mark on the observation, Dwaine had to do a PDP.

The Professional Development Plan would be like a retraining of sorts. He would have to attend educational coaching sessions, observe other teachers, write an essay on management styles, and keep a journal of all work-related experiences. In essence, it was a bunch of paperwork that came with a professional stigma that would remain with him for the rest of his life.

Under the previous principal, all of Dwaine's administrator observations had been exemplary, even though he had often demonstrated a bad habit of 'show boating' during the observations. For him, an evaluation meant it was time to add a little extra panache to his lesson. At the heart of his teaching were those 'light bulb' moments when students' eyes lit up so brilliantly he could see them beaming with pride. Making a connection with the students was of paramount importance to Dwaine.

As he walked to drop off the special needs modification forms, Dwaine thought about Ms. Lawrence's verbal tirade. Then he felt an old feeling that had once manifested in a voice motivated by his white guilt. The White Guilt Voice rolled through him. *You should have prepared that presentation. You owe them some respect.*

The Diary

Dwaine had always blamed Ms. Lawrence's bad attitude toward him on his ball cap and tattoo but that was not the whole truth. Since college he had felt uncomfortable around African Americans. It was not a matter of hate, but of shame. He could teach all races. He cared for all people. But with African Americans, he felt that he owed them something. The diary was like a thorn in his soul, a misery he longed to move past. No matter how much he prayed or meditated, his anger towards his ancestor would always eat at him.

The kids preparing for the celebration had caused Dwaine to recall a past extra credit assignment he had done in the mid-1990s during a History class he'd been taking in college. If he could bring in an artifact or relic from his family, he would get five extra points on the next test. One student had brought in a Union uniform. Another student had carried in an old pocket watch. Dwaine had brought in a daguerreotype of Edwin Mannford and a diary that he had not read. The daguerreotype was the image of a tall, gaunt old man. His great-great-grandfather had a savage look of hatred etched into his face.

The student with the Union uniform retold the story of his ancestor. The Union soldier had been at the Battle of Gettysburg and later went on to march through Georgia. The student walked around the class holding it so that everyone could see that the uniform had multiple holes of various sizes from shrapnel that had ripped through the cloth. The class asked questions about the uniform. What was the rank of the soldier? How had it been preserved? They applauded the student for having such an interesting heirloom. The student with the pocket watch gave details of its background. It was his father's watch, although it had originally belonged to his ancestor, a silversmith from the North.

Then Dwaine went to the front of the class, showed the daguerreotype picture and held up the diary. On the front cover was the family's coat of arms. He arbitrarily opened the book to a page in the middle. He had to squint to make out the old-style cursive. On page thirty-seven, he read the words out loud, feigning an exaggerated southern accent. The text would forever change his life.

Edwin Mannford's entry read, "The slaves were not able to reach their quota for the war effort today. As a result, I instructed my overseer, Kirby, to whip them all until they bled."

After reading this passage, Dwaine looked up at the class, then back down at the diary, in shock. He had read the text right. His ancestor had been a slaveholder? The professor asked him to read it again, but in a normal tone. "The slaves were not able to reach their quota for the war effort today. As result, I instructed my overseer, Kirby, to whip them all until they bled."

The professor then asked to see the diary. She read the opened page once more. "Your ancestor was a slave holder?" she asked in a curious manner.

Dwaine didn't hear a curious tone in her words, but rather a contemptuous and accusatory one. He could only nod. He grabbed the book and picture and excused himself. He could hardly breathe. He ran back to his dormitory. For hours, he could only sit in a fetal position and cry. He felt hurt, angry, and humiliated, all at once. How could his family have been involved in slavery? The next day he went to the courthouse to request a name change from Mannford to Mann. White guilt was not just some epithet. No, for him it was a cruel reality. The shame, in his mind, was deserved. It did not matter that he himself had not lived in the past. The sins of his ancestor were ever present in his mind.

The white guilt he carried kept tormenting him after that and had eventually manifested into a voice, chiding him for his privilege.

Dwaine had gone to a psychologist, whose words he recalled now. "Sometimes there are moments when you are unable to function because of this voice. You also make decisions based upon this voice. This irrational decision-making is dangerous." The psychologist told him he had an acute condition. He needed medication. A referral was made sending Dwaine to a psychiatrist, who prescribed him psychotropic medication.

Trying to escape the past, Dwaine had taken the drastic step to drop his courses at college. Before he left, he had hastily prepared a note for his long-time friend, Mei Yun, explaining his reasons for leaving school. Then he'd gone to the nearest recruitment center and signed up for the military. After serving in the military for several years, he came back to civilian life and went on to finish school to become a teacher; this time doing everything he could to avoid history courses.

He had wanted to serve others, and teaching proved to have a calming effect on him, at least at first. The prospect of getting kids to solve problems and think for themselves was an endeavor he considered fulfilling. For a period of time, at least, the White Guilt Voice had been vanquished.

Chapter Two

First Rehearsal

A small group of kids and a number of parents were busy at the after-school rehearsal, practicing speeches and tweaking presentations. Dwaine entered the bustling gym, loosening his tie from around his collar. He felt conflicted. The Black Heritage Celebration stirred up his white guilt, and he really did not want to attend. But he felt that he should. He wanted to show the kids he cared for them. At the very least, he had decided he would serve as part of the set-up crew. He rolled up his sleeves, tattoo and all, and started working with the dirty cables and wires that were lying on the ground.

This isn't my celebration. I shouldn't be here... His heart raced, numbness crept up his arm and shoulder, and the blood drained from his face. *I am such a rapscallion soul.*

Dwaine tried to escape the pain by determining what needed to be done and started working. Just as he was beginning to feel better about his contribution, the White Guilt voice spoke up in his mind. *You're a racist. You are unworthy of this celebration, Dwaine Mannford.* He resisted the thoughts.

Dwaine continued matching cords to speakers and running electrical wires to outlets. He found an audio wire running from a speaker that had been plugged into the wrong port, and he promptly changed the cords. *I'm glad I came, after all.* When all the cords had been plugged in, he wrapped tape around several bundles, so they would appear neat and orderly. No kid was going to get hurt by tripping over cords on his watch.

"Hey MJ, are you setting up the systems again?" Dwaine asked.

"Yeah, I did, but I had some sixth grade help. Why?"

"Because it's all messed up."

MJ was busy with his own work, and he dismissed Dwaine outright.

"Figures," Dwaine said to himself, then raised his voice, "Come here, MJ. You get a nuggie. Come here."

"Aw, hell no, Mr. Mann. Ain't no way you getting' me," the boy answered. He made a move to get away, but there was not much room on the twenty by twenty-foot stage filled with equipment.

"Come here." Dwaine caught MJ as he maneuvered around a large speaker and put him in a headlock. Dwaine balled his fist and raked MJ's head with his knuckles. "Do it right the first time, MJ!"

"Your pits stink, get some deodorant."

Dwaine let go. "Dang, I stink?" He looked around to see if anyone else had heard the exchange. He turned his head down to his right shoulder. He grimaced. "Crap, I do."

Before their teacher-student friendship formed, MJ, a chubby, light-skinned student, was a jerk who had bullied the Asian and white kids. Dwaine had caught him harassing a sixth grader who was a mix of black and Asian. Dwaine had reported bullying to the office, but nothing was done about it. Ms. Lawrence only reminded him of the ever-growing stack of incident reports. *So bullying is not an official offense to her*, Dwaine had thought at the time. *Racial discrimination doesn't fit the bill?* He couldn't figure out how she could be such a hypocrite. Hadn't she heard about bullying before, and how it affected students? Kids killed themselves over this kind of shit.

Dwaine had thought the best way to correct the situation would be to make a connection with MJ as an individual. Maybe he should never have tried to shove this problem off on the administration. Dwaine had found out about MJ's passion for sports and began showing up after school to shoot hoops or throw the football. The extra attention worked, and as a result, MJ quit insulting the other students.

With the music equipment set for the rehearsal, MJ said through the mic, "Everyone stand up!"

Stepping off the stage, Dwaine tried to back out of the room to let the people have their moment, but tripped on a cord and fell back. He landed near an aisle between the stands that were off to the right of the stage. Sampson Damasks, Dwaine's friend and colleague, helped him up.

"You ok?" Sampson asked.

"I'm alright," Dwaine said with a slight embarrassed feeling.

He didn't want to bring more attention to himself, so he went up half-way on the stands and sat down. He really hoped no one had seen him fall on his backside. Since people were standing in front of him, he thought he'd just sit back and let everyone enjoy the rehearsal. He noticed Ms. Lawrence looking straight at him from across the room. She was giving him a nasty look, probably because he wasn't standing.

"Damn." Dwaine rolled his eyes.

MJ gave another order, "Everyone sing our song!"

Students began to sing as the song played. All Dwaine had wanted to do was help the kids and leave without being noticed, but that was obviously not going to happen.

One girl was eyeing him with disdain. Sharia Malcolm bent towards him. "Why are you not standing, Mr. Mann?"

"I'm nice and comfy, thank you," he said, trying to speak over the music.

The ruckus attracted the attention of Aleia Jefferson, who stood on the other side of the aisle, a few rows closer to the floor. Aleia was a young lady, thirteen years old, who was dangerously thin and had a lazy left eye that drooped.

She swept back her braided hair, walked over to him and said, "Mr. Mann. Who do you think you are?"

"Look, I am leaving," he said as he stood up to walk out of the rehearsal.

Sharia didn't hold back. "You are the racist, in our school."

Aleia said, "Oh no you don't. You respect us and this song. Don't you dare walk out."

Then he heard the White Guilt Voice. *I told you. You should not be here, disrespecting them.*

Sharia cut off Aleia before she could really get started. He saw that she motioned to Aleia to move down, past a couple students, so that he couldn't hear. A group of girls followed the two as they took a couple steps away from him. They huddled together on the bleachers in front of the other students, who were still standing and singing.

All the girls looked around at each other as if deciding what they should do. Sharia paused and Dwaine strained to hear her say, "I have an idea."

Dwaine's guilt and embarrassment was too much to process. He needed to get away, so he started to walk out.

Arguing with the Boss

Ms. Lawrence made her way over to Dwaine as he was heading out the double doors.

"Mr. Mann, may I see you a moment?" she said in a tone that meant *now.*

"Sure."

"Come to my office," she demanded. "We need to come to an understanding."

"Okay." His mind raced. He groaned on the inside, annoyed that he was being called out. His annoyance turned to shame as the White Guilt Voice rose strongly in his mind and chided, *I told you to get out of that rehearsal, Dwaine Mannford.*

Dwaine made the trek with his head hung low as Ms. Lawrence led the way. She walked with a confident and disciplined stride, her head and shoulders facing forward. He was reticent and ashamed. Both of them were stone-cold silent. Several teachers and students saw them walking together and quickly stepped out of their way.

They passed a student, Ricky. "Hey Mr. Mann, how are you?" he said.

"Hey Ricky, did you win that competition?"

"Not yet. It's not till next month," he called out as he walked away.

Dwaine felt like a dog being dragged along on an invisible leash, with Ms. Lawrence yanking the chain. Once they were in her small but ornate office, several things stood out. A Persian rug was on the floor. There was a picture of her sisters, her mother, and herself smiling in a family photograph. He saw a bachelor's degree, a master's degree, and a specialist degree on the wall, hanging to the left of her desk. There was a picture of President Obama and the first lady at the 2009 Inauguration. It was positioned over her head when she sat at her desk.

"You do realize that this is a community event, don't you?" She stared at him, disdain radiating from her very being.

Dwaine was starting to get irritated. *I wish she knew the guilt I already feel. I can't tell her I am too ashamed of my ancestry.* He could only shrug at the question, blinking his eyes in bewilderment, not knowing how to respond.

He finally came up with a response. "Look, I was trying to leave. I backed up and tripped into the stands. I have no business being at your celebration."

"What do you mean?" She squinted at him. "Are you insane or just culturally insensitive?"

He started babbling, unsure of how to verbalize his emotional conflict. He repeated himself, "I really should not be there. It's your celebration."

"Mr. Mann, you need to get over it, whatever it is."

"Look, lady, I don't mind helping the kids set up, but it is a time for you and your people." *Bitch, if you only knew it was my ancestry that was causing all this.*

Ms. Lawrence was simmering, shaking her head, and looking down. She recovered her composure. "That's not the point, Mr. Mann. This might be a community celebration, but as a teacher you are required to participate in all school events. Please review your contract." Feeling that she had conquered the conversation, she continued, "Tell you what, I'll dismiss this, but you will stand with the students and show your support."

"Look, I am ashamed to be there while you and the kids are singing and celebrating." *Crap, why did that come out? She was about to let me leave.*

Dwaine was growing increasingly uncomfortable. Numbness swelled through his left shoulder and down his spine. Ms. Lawrence clenched her jaw. The flesh on her face gathered inward, pinching her nose. Hate and bitterness were forming in her expression. Her lower eyelid was twitching, her composure suddenly gone. She bit her lip and said, "Okay Mr. Mann, let me get this straight. You are ashamed of my heritage? I am going to submit an insubordination report and put it in your file. This will follow you from school to school. I promise you, you will be excluded from any promotions or transfers in the future."

"No, I meant—" he stopped. He wanted to say it, but he just couldn't do it. *I am ashamed of my ancestors.*

"Get the hell out," she said.

"Wait, please. Let me explain."

"Get out now," she stammered, pointing a finger to the door. It was all she could do to keep from slapping him.

Dwaine could not express the inner turmoil of the guilt and self-hatred that was surging through him. He started hyperventilating. *Do not show emotion.* His fear manifested in the form of pressure in his chest. He lost his breath for a moment and felt numbness in his left shoulder. He noted that he would need to ask his psychiatrist to prescribe him a higher dosage of medicine—if he survived this.

Dwaine didn't know it, but he was actually having a panic attack.

"I'm sorry. I need to apologize," he said.

"You should," Ms. Lawrence said. "Your arrogance will get you fired, and you need to learn who is in charge here."

"I do apologize, but am I correct in saying that you are threatening my career?"

"Take it how you want." Disgust speckled her words. "We are done here, Mr. Mann. Good day." She then muttered under her breath, just a little too loud, "Mr. Mann, you are marked."

He was about to leave, but the comment caused him to swivel around to face her again. "What does that mean?"

"I told you to get out!" she said, spit flying from her mouth.

"No, really. I want to know what you meant by 'you are marked.' It sounds to me as if you are threatening my livelihood."

She didn't answer. "You have ten seconds to get out of my office before I have Officer Bates escort you out of here."

"Ok, you win," he lied. He thought about taking a pill to ease the anxiety. But she was always harassing him. He was not about to let her get the better of him. He tried to remain calm, but he felt the warmth of rage swelling within him. "Please give me a moment." He tugged on the collar of his shirt.

Ms. Lawrence relaxed. She stood up and walked to the flowers on the shelf behind her. She picked up a small watering pitcher sitting next to them.

A replica baseball bat sat on the shelf next to him. She'd probably gotten it at a minor league baseball game, or maybe from a student or teacher. It didn't matter. He picked up the bat and walked to her from behind. He would end all of this for good. He was done dealing with her threats and her abuse. One, maybe two, swift strikes and she would collapse to the ground, dead. If not dead, then knocked out, unable to yell or protect herself from additional blows. He wouldn't have to put up with her anymore. She was finished.

Her hand held the small, green watering pitcher as she began to tilt it upward, allowing the last drips to fall onto the white flowers.

Just a few feet from Ms. Lawrence, Dwaine lifted the bat up and over his right shoulder. He would try to take her out in one shot. As his muscles coiled to deliver the blow, Ms. Lawrence's cell phone released a shrill tone from her jacket pocket and snapped him back into reality. Dwaine quickly brought the bat down to his side and rested it behind his leg.

Ms. Lawrence answered the call. She greeted the party on the other end and asked them to hold a moment. She turned toward him, but before she could say anything, he said, "I'm leaving." And she turned back toward the flower.

As he turned around toward the door, he slid the bat from his back to his front. Anger still poured through him, but now he was able to think through it. He would keep the bat. It was a symbol of his 'insubordination,' a word Ms. Lawrence liked to toss around. Besides, Dwaine reasoned he may need it again soon.

He could not believe that he had almost snapped. What could have possessed him? While he may have taken her bat, she most definitely had taken something of his. A part of his soul was gone, and it felt like a savage demon had taken its place.

Chapter Three

Teaching Respect

Tuesday evening, Sharia was cozying up to Samuel, lying against his chest. They were watching TV, but Samuel was really watching for his mother. She was making some cookies and had stepped out for a moment. "You're in Mr. Mann's class, right?" Sharia asked Samuel.

He looked down at her, then looked back to see if his mom was around. "Yeah, why?"

"I need you to do something for me," she said.

Her eyes were golden brown, almond shaped, and lined with makeup to accentuate their beauty. Samuel had always wanted to date Sharia, but he had never expected to get this far. She was the most popular girl in school, and he saw himself as a nobody. Even his friends had said he didn't have a chance to date her, but apparently he did. And here they were. She leaned over a little more and kissed his neck with her full lips. She turned his face and kissed him again. The feeling sent electricity through his body.

Stuttering, he straightened up and asked, "Wh... what do you need me to do?"

She took his chin to face her. "I want you to cause an accident in Mr. Mann's class."

"Why? He's pretty cool," Samuel stammered. Mr. Mann had never had a bad thing to say to him, unlike the other teachers. Mr. Mann even cut him some slack when he was late to class.

"He needs to learn some respect for other races." She looked hurt. "He didn't stand for our song during the rehearsal."

"Oh. But he seems okay. There is probably a good reason he wasn't standing," he said.

"What, you scared of him?" Sharia asked.

"No, I'm not scared of anyone."

"If you're not scared of him, I might go with you to the dance."

"Really?" Samuel asked.

"We might have some fun during the dance... And we might have some fun *after* the dance." She traced her finger around his lips and was moving in to kiss him when his mom walked into the room.

Sharia straightened up and moved away from Samuel. "There you are, Mrs. Rodriquez. How are the cookies coming? They smell delicious."

"They are not quite done, Boo," Mrs. Rodriquez said.

Samuel didn't know what to do. Mr. Mann was alright. He did require students to do a lot of work, but so did most teachers. Samuel had never had a problem with him, but Sharia was so tempting.

◆ ◆ ◆

The next day, Samuel told a couple of his closest friends that he wanted to talk to them after school. He thought he would repeat a prank that had worked for him before when he'd played a joke on a teacher in fifth grade. That shit was so funny. He had made a homemade bomb by putting an actuator next to a lighter underneath a small bag of gunpowder. With the press of a remote, the actuator caused the lighter to ignite. The gunpowder caused a small explosion. The result was an embarrassingly small bang. Nevertheless, it had sent the class into a panic. And the best thing was that he never was caught.

Samuel thought he could do the same thing by placing a bomb next to the fire extinguisher. The explosion would crack the seal and cause the fire extinguisher to blow up. No one would get hurt, and he would get the date with Sharia. Everyone would win.

Samuel thought about the chain of events needed to get the extinguisher to explode. His friends could stage a distraction on the way to lunch. Then, when Mr. Mann was preoccupied, Samuel would fit the device behind the fire extinguisher. The gunpowder and some homemade chemicals could cause a small hole in the casing. Samuel smiled. He would have easy access to it, since the wall case that held the fire extinguisher was already broken. *Lazy Picks County Fire Department*, he thought.

Jamal Wright was Samuel's best friend. Jamal had once been jumped by three kids, and during the fight, Samuel used a sharp-tipped pencil to pierce the side of one assailant. The kid had run off with the pencil still in him. Jamal was able to fight off the other kids with Samuel's help, and now he sported a scar on his cheek as a badge of honor.

DeJaun Sanchez, a quiet but moody student, could also be counted on to provide a distraction. He liked to cause chaos and point fingers. He hated school, seeing it as the white man's way to torture him. School was like jail; always stay in line, do the class work and don't speak unless spoken to. Most students were raised to respect authority and elders, but DeJaun hated saying "Sir," and "Ma'am," because the way he saw it, that would give the authority some credence. No way in the world was he going to do that, not even with his parents.

Jamal and DeJaun met Samuel after school on the dilapidated playground. "I want to pull a prank on Mr. Mann," Samuel said.

"Cool, what you wanna do?" Jamal asked. A cold and a bitter wind blew over them, and he started to rub his hands to keep warm.

Samuel thought for a moment. "You and DeJaun start a fight in the line on the way to lunch, in Mr. Mann's classroom."

A cigarette hung loosely from DeJaun's lips. He smiled and asked, "And what you gonna do?"

"I'm gonna put a bomb next to the fire extinguisher. The thing is ancient; the academy hasn't replaced it in forever. I think I could cause a rupture in the seal. The mess would go everywhere."

"It'll mess things up, that's for sure." Jamal laughed.

"When we gonna do this?" DeJaun asked.

"Tomorrow. We gonna mess that guy up," he said.

They left the playground to go to the store one block away. As they were walking, Jamal was more pensive. "Why Mr. Mann?" he questioned. "He is alright."

"Sharia said something about him learning respect. I don't know. We are going to the dance together if I make an accident happen." He continued, "I don't really want to screw with Mr. Mann, but Sharia is upset with him because he didn't stand or something, and then tried to leave during the rehearsal."

"Good 'nuff for me," Jamal said.

"I'm in," DeJaun said, taking a drag off his cigarette.

Feeling guilty, Samuel said, "Come on lets go play some video games."

The Test

The next morning, Mei Yun, Dwaine's old friend and a jaded journalist who was known for making local politicians outcasts in their own city, sat on the side of her bed pondering her dilemma. She was late. She hadn't had her period in six weeks. And she was not in good graces with her parents, due to her continual refusal to adhere to the Catholic religion. She looked over at the picture sitting on the end table of her and Sampson. They were smiling, without a care in the world. Her parents hadn't approved of their relationship, of course. Now she sat, unwed and wondering if she were about to have his child. She took the test out of the packet, trying to garner the courage to use it.

Mei contemplated possible pregnancy, agonizing over it for a while. Then she finally rose and made her way to the bathroom. She wondered what her parents will say if she were indeed pregnant. Would she bring shame to them? Of course she would; she already knew that. She paused for a moment as the thought made her look down and clasp her hands.

Damn it all! If she were pregnant, then she would be happy. But this determination was short-lived and followed by another question: How would Sampson take the news? Would he run off, not wanting to get married? How would she tell him? How would she tell her parents? Sure, she and Sampson had talked about children, but was he serious? She had been serious at times, but she had a feeling he might only be playing along for the sex.

Anxious, she entered the bathroom, took the test, and waited. It was the longest minute she had ever experienced. She closed her eyes, as the anxiety built within her mind. Her father had told her that he did not approve of her dating outside of her race. What if she had to tell him that she was pregnant with Sampson's child? She reminded herself to be positive. *Be positive*—how ironic. She tried to think of the aspects of raising a baby. The joy of having a little boy or girl and holding the baby in her arms was something she'd wanted her entire life. In her mind, she was ready for it. But was she ready to face the consequences? Could she have a successful family and a successful career? How would she juggle the two? Would she have a duty to the child above all else?

With closed eyes, she thought, *So many questions in my life. How can I face all of this with certainty*? Mei looked at a picture of her parents. A cross hung around the neck of her mother. Maybe the cross wasn't just a decoration. Maybe it was a symbol with a meaning. Maybe it leant her mother a serenity that Mei could not understand.

"One day you will take up the cross. You will still face problems, but you will not be alone. Trust me," her mother had said.

Calm returned to her. She opened her eyes. The pregnancy test had kept its promise of showing results in one minute. The symbol was... positive.

The day her mother spoke of was today. With determination and a new outlook on life, Mei picked up her phone from off the counter and called Sampson. He didn't answer, so she left both a voicemail and a text message. "We need to talk."

Faculty Meeting

Thursday Morning, the lecture room was unbearably cold—a fallout from the county cutting costs, which included heat. The room could have easily held two hundred people, but the faculty only took up a fraction of the space. It had everything that was needed for meetings: theatrical lights, visual and sound systems, and a screen descending from the twenty-foot-high ceiling. Four years ago, a local tax initiative had helped pay for the improved technology in the county schools, and as a result they were renovated with state-of-the-art media centers and lecture rooms.

As a part of the staff, Officer Bates was required to attend the faculty meeting, and Dwaine couldn't help but focus on him and Ms. Lawrence. Officer Bates was holding his stare on her like a predator waiting in high grass, biding its time to attack its prey. Ms. Lawrence stared intently back at him. Her lips stiffened as they did when she knew something was off. She had little control of the situation. Her eyes were piercing. A guilty look was plastered all over her face, and Dwaine could have seen it a mile away.

Earlier, before everyone had come to the auditorium, Dwaine had passed Ms. Lawrence in the hall and smelled a faint odor coming from her. It had seeped through her pores, most likely undetectable to her. Alcohol tended to be that way. It was like a smoker who couldn't smell the smoke.

Now Dwaine saw Officer Bates continue glaring at Ms. Lawrence, then nodded his head and stoically motion her to step aside with him. She quickly cupped her hand to her face and blew a breath up to her nostrils.

Dwaine was on the left-hand side of the auditorium, seated next to Sampson. He could not hear what was going on between the two, but it looked serious. Ms. Lawrence had called Dwaine out on many occasions, but she had never been kind enough to pull him aside first. Just like that, he felt a tinge of excitement as he realized karma was about to get her. Dwaine was pretty good at lip reading and saw Officer Bates say, "Get the drinking under control. Next time I will go through the proper channels with this."

Bates looked like he was about to go to town on her. Dwaine thought, *I bet he wishes he had a breathalyzer with him. Yeah, make her walk a straight line, Bates.*

Dwaine watched as Ms. Lawrence walked away from Officer Bates. She looked aghast. She'd been busted, and there wasn't anything she could do about it. Dwaine loved every second.

Officer Bates then turned his attention to Ms. Walker, who was known as "Screaming' Walker" to the students. Dwaine watched as the next scenario played out. Would Ms. Walker also be reprimanded? Dwaine knew what was going on with her. She was always a little too squirmy, played with her nose and was constantly sniffling as if she had a perpetual cold. Dwaine watched as Officer Bates scrutinized her. *Get her! She's a coke-head.*

Ms. Walker was struggling to open her presentation on the computer. Looking frustrated that her computer was not working, she turned to Officer Bates. "Would you mind going ahead with your comments on identifying gang activity?"

He took the mic. "Thank you for allowing me the time to speak. I would like to talk about the rise in gang activity we've seen recently at the high school. From the past, we know that once this starts at the high school, it will eventually move to the feeder school. With that in mind, I want to share with you how to spot signs of gang activity."

As Officer Bates was speaking, Sampson was doing his best to look interested in the presentation. Sitting one chair over from Dwaine, he said, "Hey Dwaine, do you think Ms.Walker is doing lines?"

"Yeah, it wouldn't surprise me." Itching, he scratched his neck. "Dang it, I had my hair cut yesterday, and I feel like I am shedding like a dog," Dwaine said as he knocked a couple hairs off his shoulder.

Mr. Hayes, an overweight social studies teacher sitting behind Dwaine, chided him, "You shed more than my Collie."

"Hey man, I need some advice. I want go out with this Chinese woman that I haven't seen in a long time. How should I approach her?" Dwaine said.

"Where does she live? Here?" Samson asked.

"She lives in the area." He paused for a moment. "Yeah, I've seen her on the news." Causally, Dwaine went on, "I've known her for years. We went to college together."

Dwaine began to reminisce about when he and Mei had met in college. She'd been in a sister sorority to his fraternity studying journalism.

They hadn't officially dated, but one time after both of them had gone out to a local pub, their drunken emotions had gotten the better of them, and they'd made out in a back storeroom. Giddy with anticipation, they'd gone to his dorm room, where they shredded their clothes and had a hot, passionate night. It might have been the best sex Dwaine ever had, but something had gone wrong that night. A sick pervert had popped open a window and stuck a video camera in the room while Dwaine and Mei were going at it. Dwaine saw the arm trying to angle the video camera to take a video. Dwaine smacked the guy's hand before he was able to record. He tried to grab the video camera, but luck was not on his side. Buck naked, he ran out of the dorm room, into the common area, and onto the balcony trying to catch the invasive interloper. The punk ran away. Dwaine could hear the peals of laughter as he ran down the stairwell. The experience sobered Mei up, and she dressed and ran to her own dorm in tears. *If only I had stopped her and calmed her down. If only...*

It was months before Mei could even talk to Dwaine, but eventually both of them became friends again. He was extremely cautious after that incident. Regret ate at him. He hated himself for putting Mei in such a compromising position.

From then on, he saw her not only as a sorority sister, but as a friend who had been wronged. They went out together as friends every now and again, but he still had deep feelings for her.

After his wife's death, he'd come to a definite decision... He wanted to start dating Mei. He hadn't seen Mei since college, but he knew from the news that she was living and working as a reporter in Statesboro.

Sampson broke Dwaine's thoughts. "I'm dating a Chinese woman who is a reporter," he said, eyeing Dwaine suspiciously.

Dwaine's mouth was agape. He was shocked to hear those words come from Sampson. *It couldn't be the same woman, could it?* Dwaine thought.

"What's her name?" Sampson asked again. "The lady you're talking about."

Their conversation was abruptly interrupted by Ms. Walker accidently sticking a cord into the wrong computer port. A loud feedback sounded over the speakers when she did. She quickly pulled it out and silenced the speaker, looking nervous and frustrated. Officer Bates had finished his presentation and stepped off to the side.

"What is her name?" Sampson was starting to look angry.

"Forget I said anything. It's nothing," Dwaine said. He was not sure if Mei was dating someone or not, but he hoped that someone was not Sampson.

"If I may have everyone's attention," Ms. Walker said, raising her voice into the microphone. "I have finally gotten the computer to work."

Dwaine and Sampson both turned toward Ms. Walker. She went down the faculty meeting agenda in a painfully slow procession.

Then a slideshow of the upcoming events, news, and policy was presented by computer illustrations. Dwaine was sarcastically appreciating the minute details going into this lecture while trying to avoid thinking that Mei and Sampson might be together. *What a beautiful way to chew us out using visual and auditory stimuli. Now all we need is a snide opinion.*

"Like hell, it's nothing." Sampson struggled to keep his voice low. "Is her name Mei Yun? Are you seeing my Mei?"

Dwaine's eyes widened at Sampson. *Shit.*

"Hey man, we're just friends." Sure, they were friends. Very good friends. But Dwaine also had very strong feelings for Mei. They had obviously, in the past, had romantic inclinations. And at some point, all of a sudden, the old feelings had come back. Dwaine had been wondering if those feelings had resurfaced in Mei as well. "You know I met her first. You should find someone else."

Ms. Walker's voice echoed through the large room. "In my opinion, a word should be said about restroom breaks."

A voice started up in Dwaine's head. *Mei Yun has been mine since college. He has only been going out with her recently. I've known her for years.*

Dwaine straightened up. The voice in his head prompted him to antagonize Sampson. *Tell him about the time you and Mei were almost caught in college.* He gave it a second thought. *I know what will really get him.*

"We were close in college, right—well actually lovers. There was this one time she thought she was pregnant; she was late. Fortunately, she took a pregnancy test and found out she wasn't. We stayed friends afterward," Dwaine said.

Ms. Walker turned around to see Mr. Turner entering through one of the double doors. The man was usually dapper and debonair, but today he was a mess and coming in late. He was smiling from ear to ear and his shirt looked like it had been hastily tucked in.

"Uh, sorry for the delay, we had some projects we were working on," he said apologetically, trying to turn the attention away from himself.

Touching the calloused part of her nose next to the nostril, Ms. Walker said, "Sit down and be quiet."

"You screwed my Mei?" Sampson could barely control himself. "Mei and I have been dating for a long time."

"Hey don't worry about it. It's in the past. Focus on the here and now. Plus, I don't think Mei would call it screwing." *You think you have been dating her for a long time?*

Sampson was fidgeting in his seat. "You can't ask her out," he finally blurted out.

"Hell yeah," Dwaine said. "You know why she's dating you, right?" He paused. "She feels sorry for you, and by the look of it I'd say that's about right," he said, continuing to antagonize Sampson. Mei was his, and he'd decided to let Sampson know it.

Ms. Walker was still talking, "Concerning the Equal Skills Curriculum, there are academic policies that will be changing. When a student gets an answer wrong, but can explain why it is correct, you are to give that student credit," she said in a contemptuous tone.

Mr. Smith spoke up. "I'm sorry, Ms. Walker. Can you repeat that?"

She did not look at him, but simply went on, "It is a new policy."

Some teachers sighed, resigned to their students' educational fate. They probably figured that two or three years from now this policy would change again, just like all the others.

Screw with Sampson, a voice whispered in Dwaine's head. "Hey Sampson, does she do that little thing with you?"

"What little thing?" Sampson said, way too loud for a faculty meeting.

Dwaine knew Sampson tended to get a little loud when he was emotional, and his behavior now was no different.

"Oh, never mind," Dwaine said. "I guess she is out of her kinky phase."

"Fuck you!" Sampson tried to keep his voice from getting loud, worried that the administrators might hear him. Some people looked at him.

Dwaine just shrugged.

At the front of the auditorium, it looked like Ms. Walker had heard what Sampson had said. "Is there a problem, Mr. Damasks? Can we have your attention? We are having a faculty meeting here," she said out loud.

Sampson looked like he wanted to bite her head off, but he simply said, "Sure, Ms. Walker. Sorry for the interruption."

Ms. Walker withdrew her death stare and continued, "Next, the federal government specifically the Department of Education and Department of Justice has sent all the schools and the county school board members a letter stating that they want to see equality in discipline."

"We are going to have a talk about this later, Dwaine," an irate Sampson muttered.

Mr. Smith blurted out, "What does 'equality in discipline' mean?"

Ms. Walker looked down her nose and said, "Mr. Smith, review the protocols for the faculty meetings and raise your hand. It means that you teachers will be taking into account the race of the students when disciplining them."

"Please elaborate," Mr. Smith returned.

"The president's administration has become concerned with the inequality of student discipline." She continued, "Students who are minorities are being written up a lot more than *other* students. When you find yourself about to write up a student, ask yourself the following questions: Why am I writing this child up? Is it due to race?" She went on, "Remember, it is your task to keep students working. When a student misbehaves, it means that you were unable to connect with that student."

Numerous teachers shifted uncomfortably in their seats.

Ms. Walker continued, "Inequality is noticeable in office referrals, as evidenced by the fact that not all races are proportionately represented in the in-school suspension room. This is something that we truly have to address in order to bring equality to the academy. Govern yourselves accordingly."

A chirp came from Sampson's pocket. It was his voicemail. He looked around and saw that Ms. Walker was not facing him. He heard another sound.

Sampson, unconcerned with what the text meant, showed it to Dwaine to get in his own jab. It was a text message. 'We need to talk,' it said. "I told you we're dating. Don't you dare come between Mei and me."

Dwaine felt tightness in his chest when he saw the message. An older version of Mei's picture was next to the text. Talk about what? The Voice spoke to him again. *You can't let him take her.*

At that point, Dwaine wanted to just reach out and slam the phone into Sampson's face. He needed his medicine. He couldn't focus on anything else. Mei Yun was his.

"Aw, hell no," Dwaine said to Sampson.

"Find another woman."

Catching air in his throat, Dwaine started to stutter but finally composed himself the best he could. "Like hell. She's only with you because she doesn't know that I want her," Dwaine finally confessed.

Ms. Walker raised her voice over the mic again. "Next on the agenda, the Superintendent and Assistant Superintendent will be coming and interviewing students to find out how they feel about the academy. Several parents have been asked to interview with them as well."

Dwaine winced when Ms. Walker yelled in his direction in her tense, high-pitched voice.

"The last point on the agenda is to address the Black Heritage Celebration to be held in honor of Black History Month," Ms. Walker said. She continued, "Students will dress up for the occasion and that means you should too."

The White Guilt Voice echoed in Dwaine's mind. *Hey Mannford, Dwaine Mannford. You should not be there!*

Leave me alone! He told himself internally, the words playing off his lips. He glanced around the room to see if anyone had noticed his lips moving, worried that he might give someone the wrong impression.

"All hearts and minds clear?" Ms. Walker asked.

No one answered. "Good, we are all in agreement. Have an educational day."

"I heard you got into it with Ms. Lawrence again. You are upsetting all kinds of people, including me," Sampson said as he started to get out of his chair.

Dwaine's retort was swift. "Screw off. You'll be sorry when Mei and I are together."

As the two men reached the hallway and most teachers were going in the opposite direction, they stepped behind an open door. Sampson grabbed Dwaine and pushed him against the wall. "This is not over, Dwaine" he growled.

Dwaine replied, "She is mine."

Ms. Lawrence overheard the two as she was making her way to the water fountain and looked at them. "What is going on?" she said.

Looking back at Ms. Lawrence, Sampson said, "Err nothing ma'am," and released Dwaine's shirt.

Dwaine stood and watched Sampson walk away. His heart raced as his ire grew. He felt like he was entering a dark tunnel.

Chapter Four

Dress Rehearsal

Later Thursday morning, Dwaine was walking down the hall towards the gym to listen to the sound equipment. Beads of sweat ran down his neck and forehead. Maybe it was Mei and Sampson that was bothering him. Maybe it was the upcoming celebration. Whatever it was, he found himself taking the longest route to get to the gym. Coming to the corner of another hall, he stopped when he saw Ms. Walker enter her office.

A moment later, he saw Ms. Lawrence approach from a different direction and walk into Ms. Walker's office, leaving the door partially opened. She must have thought everyone was in the gym or their classrooms. Dwaine quietly stepped to the door and eased his head around to peer inside.

"Sylvia Willis had an issue the other day with a student coming to her home," Ms. Lawrence said.

"Run that by me again," Ms. Walker said.

"One of Sylvia's students, Mickey Strickland, went to her home the other day. I think the boy proposed to her or something. It was pretty ugly."

"Where is he now?" Ms. Walker said.

"Youth Detention Center," Ms. Lawrence said.

"Oh boy," Ms. Walker said, "We are going to have to see about an alternative arrangement for him. There'd be no sense in keeping him near Sylvia. But now we have a rehearsal to oversee," she said with a big smile.

"Wait, before we leave I want to know when we are going to start issuing contracts," Ms. Lawrence asked.

"Probably next month," Ms. Walker said. "Why?"

"I think we should rethink Mr. Mann's renewal. I have someone in mind to take his place."

"He is an odd one. Some of the parents don't like him either," Ms. Walker said. "Come on, let's go."

Dwaine quickly stepped away and turned a corner down another hallway. *Great, I am getting the fucking axe.*

Once at the gym, Ms. Walker climbed onto the stage and called for everyone's attention. Several classes had been called there to act as the attending crowd. MJ requested that everyone stand to sing. While taking a quick look at the cords and listening to the quality of the sound, Dwaine became uncomfortable and turned red. He quickly moved to the seats. Not only had he just found out that he'd soon be losing his job, but his white guilt was plaguing him. Nonetheless, he stood up and started to sing along.

What are you doing standing here?

Dwaine fought back against the White Guilt Voice, answering it, *The right thing.*

Dwaine Mannford, your family enslaved these people. An image flashed in his mind of slaves working in a field under the watchful eye of his ancestor. Dwaine was in the second row of stands. He suddenly couldn't take it anymore. He sat down. He was sweating, and his heart was racing. He looked up and saw Ms. Lawrence eyeing him. The students were still standing and singing.

"Mr. Mann, you're supposed to be standing," Samuel said.

Dwaine looked up with red eyes. "Screw off, kid. Leave me alone."

"Crazy teacher," DeJaun, who was right next to Samuel, mumbled under his breath.

Dwaine had to give the students credit. The song was beautiful, and the kids were putting their hearts into singing it. It was an inspiring moment and Dwaine wished he could get past his guilt and share in it.

A tear streamed down his face. Then he saw Mrs. Howard coming down the aisle towards him. *Did she see me crying?* She stopped beside where he was seated and turned towards him. *Why?* He wondered. She sang with all her heart. He looked up at her. As she continued to sing, she looked down at him and offered a hand. *Does she know about my family?* He thought while admiring her voice. She sounded like an angel. Mrs. Howard stretched her arm out farther towards him.

"You don't understand," he said with regretful eyes.

"You're right, I don't. But whatever it is, you will overcome it. Now rise and sing with me," she said, and then began singing again.

He took her hand, stood up, and tried to sing. His inflection was off, his tone was terrible, and he did not know the lyrics.

"Sing..." He fumbled with the words.

"You are doing fine. Keep singing."

"... Of hope," she sang.

"... Hope," Dwaine tried to join in.

His mind cleared and, for a brief moment, he was at peace.

Lunch Time

Back at class, Dwaine tried to focus during the introductory writing exercise. The topic today was 'Should the United States fight with Turkey against Russia?' *What kind of question is this?* Dwaine shook his head, irritated.

"What in the world does the military have to do with business class?" one of the kids asked, half joking and half serious. The children were giddy in anticipation of the upcoming celebration and did not want to work.

Dwaine answered the question by asking another one. "You know, I am still trying to figure that out. But the county wants all the schools to be on the same page. So what do you think? Should the U.S. stick up for Turkey?"

"No way!" one of the girls squealed out. "Why should we stick up for a bird?"

Dwaine rolled his eyes and slowly looked around.

"I'm not writing about that, Mr. Mann. I am writing about Black History Month."

One of the other kids chimed in, "Hey, Mr. Mann, I didn't know you could sing."

"Yeah, me neither. Weird isn't it?" he reflected. "I guess if you have the right motivation—maybe the right person with you—you can do just about anything," he admitted begrudgingly to the student.

"You know, Mr. Mann, she is married," the kid said, teasing his teacher.

"You just had to go there, didn't you?" Dwaine said through a half-cocked smile. The power of acceptance was inspiring.

"Sure did!" The student giggled at Dwaine.

"I would hate to get all sentimental on you all," Dwaine said, trying to ignore the remarks. He checked his watch. "Alright people, let's work on our individual module activities."

Most students were writing about Black History Month or practicing their parts and did not want to start on the lesson. While walking around, Dwaine was amused that a group of students were taking images of rappers and adding audio from other songs. He stopped to watch. *At least they were being imaginative.* He moved on to a particularly mischievous student. She had taken the tune 'Mary had a Little Lamb' and edited it to a country singer's performance. *It's funny, and I have to give her credit for creativity.*

One student, Marcus, stopped Dwaine as he passed by and asked, "Mr. Mann, do you like crackers?"

Dwaine's eye twitched and he pursed his lips together, starting to ball up his fist. But then he remembered these were children, and they didn't know any better. They needed a role model for behavior, not some hot-headed jerk. He counted silently for a moment, letting out deep breaths. Calming down, he said, "No, Marcus, and I don't like the crackers with my soup either. Now, real talk: Would you like for me to make racial jokes? I bet not. So please, let's keep class professional. Are we good?"

"We're straight, Mr. Mann. Just messing with you," Marcus said, still grinning but looking slightly embarrassed.

"Kids," Dwaine said to himself. Hate them for a moment and best buds the next. As jaded as he was about his superiors, Dwaine always tried to maintain a positive attitude with his students.

Twenty-five minutes later, Dwaine looked at Samuel and wondered why he was making a funny sign. *Must be a new signal gangs are using. Wait a minute, is Samuel in a gang*?

About that time, Dwaine announced, "Ok class, lunch time. Girls line up first, please." Once the girls were in formation, Dwaine said, "Ok boys, go ahead and get behind them. It's chow time."

As the thirty-five students lined up and started to walk out, Jamal and DeJaun started arguing.

"We are going to tear them up on Sunday," Jamal started. "They suck."

"You don't know what you're talking about," DeJaun retorted, pushing Jamal.

Dwaine couldn't tell if they were playing or not. *Damn, aren't they friends?*

Jamal shoved back at DeJaun and Dwaine said in an even tone, "Stop it, boys."

Dwaine moved towards the action, but he felt someone bump into him.

"Sorry, Mr. Mann," Samuel said.

Dwaine turned his attention back toward the fight. Students had circled around the two boys, who had begun to wrestle. One of the students closest to the fight started a play-by-play commentary using his phone as a mic.

The students were yelling, "Mess him up! Get 'em." They didn't seem to have a favorite, but just wanted to egg the two on. A couple of students were videotaping the fight from their phones. It was sure to show up on social media.

"Aww crap, this is getting serious now," Dwaine said under his breath. He caught the arm of one of his best students and told her to go get an administrator.

Before she had a chance to go, Samuel stepped beside Dwaine and yelled, "Jamal, DeJaun, cut it out! Let's go to lunch." The two immediately stopped fighting and bumped fists.

Dwaine looked at Samuel, who rolled his eyes and said, "Kids, these days."

However, the department chair for electives teachers, Mr. Jenkins, had been on the way to lunch with his class and had heard the altercation. He barked out the order, "Students, line up against the wall. We'll go to lunch in a minute."

Mr. Jenkins was one of the coaches for the boys, and his athletes snapped to attention immediately. He asked, "Mr. Mann is everything ok?"

"Sure. The kids are friends, but they were fighting over next Sunday's game," Dwaine said. "The stupid things students fight over..." Dwaine was confused.

"Take our brawlers to the office and let the administration deal with them," Mr. Jenkins said. "I'll take your students to lunch with me. See you there."

When Dwaine arrived at the office with Jamal and DeJaun, Ms. Lawrence was there and was visibly upset. Some test scores had come in, and they were not good.

Dwaine pointed to a row of chairs against the wall and said, "Sit there, boys."

"What's the matter now, Mr. Mann?" Ms. Lawrence asked.

Dwaine went through the details of how he and his class were on the way to lunch when a fight broke out between the boys over a game.

"I have a lot of paperwork, dealing with a variety of incidents. Why did you allow the boys to fight?"

Dwaine knew he couldn't say anything, since the fight had happened on his watch. It occurred to him then that administrators don't want problems. They see any classroom flaw as a direct tarnish on the teacher. *Keep your mouth shut and take it.*

"You have to keep these students engaged in academics, Mr. Mann. Now go do your freaking job!"

Dwaine just shook his head and left. "Come on, boys. Let's go."

Dwaine sulked his way back to the lunch room with Jamal and DeJaun in tow. He heard sounds of a fight in the girl's restroom as they passed by. He figured they were 'running the thirty,' a gang initiation. Students were beaten up for thirty seconds to see if they were tough enough for gang membership. It was a common occurrence at the school.

"Figures," he mumbled to himself. "I've had enough of fights today." He banged on the door and announced himself. Silence followed. The door opened and five girls filed out with their heads held low, trying to hide their identities. Dwaine's stomach growled. "Good thing for you, I'm hungry."

♦ ♦ ♦

Samuel looked around to make sure Mr. Mann was not close by. Concerned, he turned to his friends Jeremiah, Marcus, and Jose. "You all sit near the wall with the fire extinguisher, right?" An introverted student, Tyler, whose father was a science teacher at the high school, sat to the far right of Samuel. He didn't say anything, just ate his food and listened.

"Yeah, why?" Jeremiah asked.

"When we get back to class, you stay away from that wall."

"Why? I like playing video games over there," Jose said.

"Just trust me," Samuel said. "We are going mess things up in Mr. Mann's class."

Incoming

The students were relatively quiet going back to class. For once, they were moving on their own and didn't have to be coerced to form a line or keep going, even as they stopped at the restrooms. While Dwaine internally commended their orderly actions, he actually wondered what was going on. *Sure wish it could be like this all the time.*

♦ ♦ ♦

Samuel was the last to return from the bathroom break. He filed in behind the others and sat down, looking around to see if anyone was watching. He reached into his backpack and retrieved the remote control to the bomb. He felt his stomach turn. For a moment, he hesitated, but just couldn't help himself. *For Sharia.* He slid the remote under his arm, so it was covered and pointed it at the fire extinguisher.

Click. The actuator depressed the lighter, igniting the gunpowder. There was a loud *boom.* As the gunpowder exploded, it damaged the seal on the fire extinguisher. An explosion followed as the fire extinguisher shot out of the case like a rocket, bursting into the wall. The sound echoed down the hall. Foam was everywhere. Some students hit the floor while others just sat in their seats, wide-eyed. After the initial shock had worn off, the kids started yelling and screaming.

Dwaine looked around and said, "Anyone hurt?" He continued, "What the hell happened?" He usually didn't use profanity in front of the students, but under these circumstances it had just slipped out.

Dwaine raised his voice. He didn't like it when his students ignored him, especially when danger was involved. "I said, is everyone okay?"

"Yes, Mr. Mann," said some students who were looking around. Many others were still cowering.

A minute later, Ms. Lawrence and Ms. Walker burst into the room. *Oh, damn,* he thought. *That didn't take long.* The two went to work assessing the situation. They saw the black powder burns on the wall where the fire extinguisher used to rest. It was obvious that this was no accident.

Ms. Walker swung around and questioned harshly, "Which one of you knows about this?"

Ms. Lawrence joined the interrogation. "Someone did this. Now who was it?" As she scanned the room of students, one eye twitched repeatedly.

Ms. Walker pulled a clipped radio from her waistband and called for the janitor.

Ms. Lawrence said, "Ok then, we will do an investigation of the whole class."

Samuel turned red and began fidgeting nervously. He held his head down and shuffled his feet uncontrollably. He was not his jaunty self. He would normally take advantage of the turmoil to make jokes.

"What is going on?" Ms. Lawrence asked him. "You act like you had something to do with this."

Samuel looked down and just stuttered, "Nothing."

Not having anything to go on, she eyed him suspiciously and said, "Alright."

The janitor made it to the room and started to clean.

"Mr. Mann, take your students to the auditorium. We will convene this afternoon," Ms. Walker said.

The students lined up and left, except for one boy, Tyler, who hung back. "Ms. Lawrence, I want to tell you something."

"Did you do this?"

"No Ma'am, but I have an idea of who did," Tyler said. "At lunch, Samuel was telling the other boys to keep their heads down."

"Was he?"

"He said that things were going to get messed up," Tyler said.

"Thank you, child," she said, "Now go to the auditorium."

Student Investigation

Ms. Lawrence walked with Ms. Walker briskly to the auditorium.

Once there, Ms. Walker said in the most serious voice the students had likely ever heard, "Samuel, we need to have a talk. Now."

Samuel tried to brush it off in front of the rest of the class as he left with them. Once they were outside with the door shut, Ms. Walker grabbed him by the arm, lifting him up as he tried to walk.

"What did I do?" he asked.

"You know damn well what you did," Ms. Lawrence said.

Ms. Walker followed up by saying, "We want to know why."

Just then her radio sounded with Mrs. Crabapple's voice, the academy's secretary and receptionist. "Ms. Walker, there is a call from Mr. Nicholas."

Ms. Walker rolled her eyes.

"Shall I tell him that you will call back later?" Mrs. Crabapple asked.

"I can handle this, Ms. Walker," Ms. Lawrence said.

"No, I will be right there, Mrs. Crabapple," Ms. Walker said, then released Samuel and left him with Ms. Lawrence.

As the two of them walked down the hall, Ms. Lawrence asked, "What's this, Samuel?" A remote control was loosely hanging out of his side pocket. "Why do you have a remote control in your pocket?" she said as she took it. Samuel didn't answer.

Once they were in her office, Ms. Lawrence said, "Come clean about the incident."

Samuel crossed his arms. "I didn't have anything to do with the bomb," he said.

"How do you know it was a bomb?" She paused. "Tell me now. If not, we will investigate. If you had a hand in it, we will get Officer Bates to arrest you for vandalism, destruction of school property, and endangering children."

Samuel was silent.

"Well?" She raised an eyebrow. "We also have a witness from the lunch room. He says you told the boys to keep their head down."

As no confession was forthcoming, Ms. Lawrence took out her radio. "Officer Bates, please come to Ms. Lawrence's office."

"Ok, wait, I was involved. I set the whole thing up," Samuel said sullenly. "I put a homemade bomb next to the fire extinguisher."

"Why?" she asked.

"I just wanted a date with Sharia."

◆ ◆ ◆

It was only a minute later that an announcement blared over the intercom, "Sharia Malcolm, come to Ms. Lawrence's office. Sharia Malcolm, come to Ms. Lawrence's office immediately."

When Sharia arrived, she saw Samuel sitting in a chair with a dismal look on his face.

Ms. Lawrence cut to the chase. "Have a seat. Samuel and I have just had an interesting discussion. He told me that you had a hand in an incident today."

"What incident?" she asked with as much innocence as she could muster.

"Don't you play coy with me, young lady," Ms. Lawrence retorted and leaned forward. "You best come clean before I deal with you in a harsh manner."

"Oh, you mean that loud sound earlier?" Sharia dropped her head and then cut her eyes to Samuel.

Ms. Lawrence reached for the radio and said, "Officer Bates, what is your location?"

Officer Bates said, "I will be there shortly. I am in the gym."

She looked at Sharia. "You were saying?"

"Okay, okay, I told Samuel that I would go to the dance with him if he would cause problems in Mr. Mann's class."

"So you had a hand in it?" Ms. Lawrence asked.

"Well, yeah," Sharia smugly admitted.

"Why would you put him up to a prank like that?" Ms. Lawrence was disgusted with the girl.

"Mr. Mann would not stand for our song."

"So you goaded Samuel into causing damage to school property? You felt the need to have a whole class of students put in danger over your pride?" It began to make sense now. Ms. Lawrence understood why the two boys had fought before lunch. "So, Samuel, you set up the fight between Jamal and DeJaun today, so you could make your move, right? Am I missing anything?" Ms. Lawrence asked with a sharp edge to her voice. Her anger was not so much directed at the students as much as it was at Mr. Mann for creating an environment that had caused so much resentment. Ultimately, in her eyes, he had caused the fight and the explosion. It was all Mr. Mann's fault for being insensitive at the rehearsal. Still, the damage could have been far worse.

Sharia looked up at Ms. Lawrence and blurted out, "We were just trying to teach the man a lesson about respect."

Ms. Lawrence glared at Sharia. "Let me tell you something about respect. We respect ourselves when we respect others. To take out your anger on others is disrespectful as well, especially when you involve friends and classmates. Whatever reason Mr. Mann had for not standing up, you should not use his behavior as an excuse to go ballistic and put others in danger. The ignorant will eventually get what they deserve, so hold yourself to a higher standard. You must act with class when others do not. This is what it means to have pride. Do you understand?"

"Yes Ma'am, I think so," Sharia said, hanging her head a little lower than before.

Ms. Lawrence recalled the government's letter she had received about racial equality when disciplining students and made up her mind what the punishment would be. She also knew that Mr. Mann had, in fact, engendered an environment of distrust and anger. She shuddered anew at her own anger over that incident. He was the only man she knew that was so purposefully insensitive to the needs of others. "Sharia," she said firmly, "You are going to wash tables in the lunch room for the next week. You are dismissed."

Ms. Lawrence looked over to Samuel, who was sitting in the seat next to the door. She sighed as Sharia exited her office. Then she dealt with Samuel. "Samuel, you have In-School Suspension for two days."

He had to know this was only a slap on the wrist, and he offered no resistance.

"Your suspension starts immediately. Go and report to Mr. Simon."

"Yes, Ma'am," Samuel said, almost gleefully.

Blame the Teacher

"Mr. Mann, report to Ms. Lawrence's office." The announcement blared over the P.A. system.

Five minutes later, Dwaine arrived. He had barely made it through the door before Ms. Lawrence began, "I've discovered the cause of the recent disruption in your classroom. You offended Sharia Malcolm during a rehearsal. She put Samuel up to the task of making a bomb and set it next to the fire extinguisher. Suffice it to say, I have dealt with the students involved."

"Good," he said.

She went on, "I've also determined that you have been grossly incompetent. You have created an environment of hatred among the students. You were not respectful of the multicultural environment at the academy, you wore an inappropriate hat in the school, and your tattoo is very offensive to the faculty. Ultimately, you have created an unsafe environment in the classroom that has endangered your students."

"What?" Dwaine was exasperated.

"You are to take unpaid leave for two days. You should also reconsider your options here at the academy."

"Let me get this straight. Multiple students plan and conspire to pull a dangerous prank—set off a bomb, no less—and I am being blamed and punished?"

"Mr. Mann—" Ms. Lawrence started to reply but was abruptly cut off.

"I am not done. How about we inform the association of this shit?" He was not part of any association, but she didn't know that. "Then, how about we inform the press about how you treat teachers and students?" He continued the rant, unable to control himself verbally, "How about we inform the media?" Taking a moment to try to calm down, he continued, "I'm sure the county would like another black eye. I know how you administrators like to deal with things. I've had enough and am about to get very nasty with this."

She said in a slow and deliberate tone, "You allowed a dangerous situation to occur. A teacher's job is to inspire and educate. We are done here."

A voice shot through Dwaine's head. *She is going to get you fired.* It wasn't the White Guilt Voice this time. It was the vicious and savage voice, the same one that had antagonized him over Sampson. *You can't let her do this to you. You must fight her now.*

"So you are saying it is entirely the teacher's fault for this? I am to blame? I planned this? I carried it out? Is that what you're saying?" He continued, "Oh, and by the way, this is being recorded to send to my friends in the news... and I am not taking leave." He pulled his phone out of his pocket. He was barely able to think rationally at this point.

You need to hurt her. Hurt her now.

Instinctively, he reached to his lower back where he often kept a gun when he wasn't at work, but he realized there was no firearm there.

"Pretty pathetic, Mr. Mann."

The pain in his chest started to rise and numbness set in from the right side of the brain to his shoulder.

Hit her. Strangle her. The Voice was prodding him to take action. *She deserves some pain. She will never stop.* He felt justified in his anger. An image of him standing over Ms. Lawrence with both hands around her neck formed in his mind. *She doesn't respect you. Squeeze the life out of her now!*

The ire rose in Dwaine and his vision became fuzzy. Although it was difficult to focus, he cast his eyes on Ms. Lawrence in a menacing stare. He took a step towards her. His jaw was set, his face emotionless.

Ms. Lawrence stood up and took a step back to match his threatening step forward. "What are you doing?" she asked, obviously shaken up. This was the first time Dwaine had ever seen fear in the woman's eyes.

Dwaine's vision deteriorated to a dangerous point; he was about to blackout. He was feeling his muscles tensing up like those of a panther about to pounce. That is when he heard a sharp knock at the door. The secretary needed to see Ms. Lawrence immediately. The sound snapped him back to reality, but he didn't entirely understand what had happened.

He thought to himself, *these emotions do not control me.* He centered himself and regained control. His heart rate began to slow. *I am better than that.*

Once his breathing slowed, Dwaine pointed to his phone and said, "I am not taking leave. The students caused this. They planned it." He pressed 'save' on his phone. "For now, I'm saving the conversation."

"Get out." Ms. Lawrence sat down and began nervously ruffling through paperwork.

Dwaine left the office in a huff. *What a bitch,* he thought. The pressure in his chest began to mount again. *Not another panic attack!* "I need a drink, maybe some more pills," he said to himself.

As Dwaine walked down the hall towards his classroom, hurt feelings surfaced. This experience had felt the same when he caught his ex-wife with her lover. What could he do to move past the pain?

A twisted smile turned up one edge of Dwaine's face. He would just have to help karma out a little bit. He would not commit or condone violence, but it had to be something to get people's attention and her attention. It had to be something to shame her.

Chapter Five

Spite

Prior to school release, Dwaine couldn't shake the events of the day. His mind obsessed over the kids' prank, the meeting with Ms. Lawrence, and over Mei. Pain rose in his chest. His heart beat faster. *Think of something, quick.*

He had to get his mind off the pain. He needed revenge... on Ms. Lawrence, Sampson, Samuel, and Sharia. He wanted to keep his schemes innocuous. What could he do? He struggled with how wrong it would be, but he figured that they needed to pay somehow. The thought of getting even made the pain subside.

Suddenly, the Voice grabbed his attention. *You must punish her. You must punish all of them.* A similar emotion arose, like it had in Ms. Lawrence's office. But something was different. There was no pressure, no pain now. He was calm. Why? Did revenge make him feel better? In any case, it was a welcome relief from the White Guilt Voice.

He rose from his desk to walk around the room. *I should probably see the doctor again. I need more medicine. Something,* he thought. Pain shot through him at the thought. He hated the medicine that he had to take to control the two voices. *Voices?* There were two distinct voices—now.

The Savage Voice spoke. *This is between me, you, and those jerks. Junior, you are going to get revenge. You are going to scare the shit out of Ms. Lawrence and those punk kids.*

Dwaine regained some control over his thinking. *I am not hurting anyone.* He concentrated on his thoughts and struggled to take them back.

People only respect the strong. We should get some guns.

No guns, Dwaine mentally replied to the Savage Voice. Then he thought of the rodents, skunks, and snakes that he often saw in the neighborhood. Looking at his tattoo of the coiled snake, he said, "I know Ms. Lawrence doesn't like snakes."

You got it, the voice spoke with conviction.

Still looking at the tattoo, he read aloud the inked text, "Don't tread on me."

Now you're talking.

"How does one go about capturing snakes?" he asked himself. "Yeah, that is exactly what I'm going to do. Scare the shit out of her. That will teach that bitch a lesson."

More vengeful ideas and images flooded Dwaine's mind. *After that, you have to get everyone's attention.* A sly smile crept over his mouth. *You could set off a bomb in a vacated room. You have a gun; just wave it around. You can shoot it while no one is looking.*

"No violence, but I have an idea," he said to himself. He thought, *doesn't she have a wedding coming up or something?*

I think so, but first we have something else to do, the Savage Voice said.

Goodbye Love

Thursday afternoon, the Savage Voice was directing Dwaine's body. He knew he couldn't match Sampson's strength in an outright fight. What could he do to even the odds? Planning was needed.

He would have to use the element of surprise. Next, to cover his tracks in case of an investigation, he was going to need to lead suspicion away from Dwaine. In a nearby town, Emerson, fifteen miles away, paying in cash, he bought a pair of boots two sizes too big.

He left his car at an empty lot in a neighborhood far from Sampson's house. Carrying his duffle bag, he walked towards the house. Looking around, he saw that no one was paying him any attention. At the house and through a window, he saw Sampson drinking in the kitchen. Instead of entering through the garage door, he would try going around to the front door to get the drop on him. He quickly picked the locks with a torsion wrench, and pushing on the door slightly, he entered.

◆ ◆ ◆

Sampson arrived home and found a note from Mei Yun taped to the door.

"My love, I have a surprise for you," the note said.

Thinking he was going to hear that she had received a raise or promotion, he retrieved a bottle from the wine rack, took a glass out of the cabinet and filled it.

He took a sip and said to himself, "Baby, I have a surprise for you too." He released a devilish grin as he undressed with Mei in mind.

Sampson's celebratory moment didn't last long. The thought of seeing Mei automatically sparked the memory of his previous conversation with Dwaine. The thought caused his brow to cave into a scowl.

He turned the glass of wine up and drained it, immediately grabbing the bottle to fill it again. Sips turned into gulps until half the bottle had been quickly emptied. The rush of alcohol only increased his anger and darkened his thoughts. After draining the third glass, Sampson began pacing and talking out loud. "Has Mei been seeing him behind my back? Maybe that's what she wants to talk to me about." He poured another glass until it was full, leaving only a small amount remaining in the bottle. He emptied it in several large swallows and wiped his mouth with his white shirt sleeve, leaving large stains on his shirt from the red liquid. He turned the bottle up and the last of the wine ran down his face. "Ah, hell no! She has been cheating on me with Dwaine." Leaving the empty bottle on the table, he grabbed another from the wine rack.

He had only just begun to twist the corkscrew into the cork when he heard the front door creak. He left the wine glass on the table and said, "You're late. Where have you been?" He fumed at the thought that Mei could have been with Dwaine.

There was no answer.

"Mei? I asked you, where have you been?" He took long, purposeful strides from the kitchen, bottle in hand, down the short hall and into the living room. He was ready to fight. Ready to fight with Mei.

There was no answer and no one in the room.

"Mei, damn it, stop screwing around. Have you been sleeping with Dwaine Mann? Where are you?"

Sampson's mind spun in a whirlwind of anger and excessive wine. Then he heard the soft approach of footsteps from behind him, but before he could turn around, a hand grasped his chin and pulled his head up and back, exposing his neck. The knife quickly went across his throat.

"She is mine," a malicious voice said. Though his head was tilted up, Sampson tried to look down and back. He grimaced as the sound of sliced muscle and cartilage ended with a feeling of warm blood. The bottle dropped. Blood poured down his neck, soaking his shirt. Sampson tried to struggle, but the attack had been too fast, and he was too drunk. Blackness fell over his tormented mind. Sampson Damasks never saw his attacker, nor would he ever see his beloved Mei again.

♦ ♦ ♦

Dwaine's face was filled with contempt and disdain. The Savage Voice peered down and saw that blood had smeared on his shirt. Standing in the living room, he realized that he had stepped in blood, leaving a distinct print on the carpet. He was prepared. He pulled out a pair of new wet-shoes from his bag. He then took out a new shirt and put the blood-stained one, the boots and the knife in a trash bag. He then put the trash bag and the contents into his duffle bag. Before leaving the house, he resisted the urge to spit on the corpse.

The Savage Voice, in control of Dwaine's body, went to a gas station in another county and dumped the trash bag into a trashcan.

The Plan

Waking up on a couch with the wet-shoes still on, Dwaine did not remember arriving home from the academy. *What the hell are those doing on my feet? I haven't been kayaking in years.* What he did remember was his need for a beer, and his plan to devise a way to capture a snake. Shaking the confusion off, he searched the internet for 'catching snakes.' He made a list of materials he would need: snake tube, gloves, snake-proof boots, and a hook-stick.

"I really should not be doing this," Dwaine mumbled to himself. As soon as the words passed his lips, he felt a sharp pain tear through the left side of his brain.

You will do this. You will make her pay. Dwaine straightened up as if he had been called out by a commanding general.

He tried to inject reasoning into the conversation with his Savage Voice. *You're talking about terrorizing a woman.*

So, she is a tough woman. She doesn't get rattled easily.

◆ ◆ ◆

It didn't take long for Dwaine to locate the nest of snakes at the edge of the subdivision.

He took a small, red-colored firecracker, lit the short fuse, and dropped it into the hole. It went off with a *pop*. Two snakes with odd-looking tails came out of the hole immediately. One looked like it had black soot on it.

The snakes were making a funny sound. *Good. Those are rattlers.* He got the hook-stick up under the snake's body and quickly backed away. The snake was trying to bite at him but he kept it at bay, although he lost track of the other snake in the process. Keeping an eye on his prey, he lifted the snake into the tube. The second rattler slithered behind him, coiled up, and attacked him. It aimed for his calve, but its fangs met the hard plastic that protected Dwaine's legs. Feeling the bump against his shin, Dwaine looked down, raised his heel, and brought it down on the snake's head. *Crack*. He carried his catch to the house and carefully stored it in the garage. He went into the house to clean up and plan his next move.

He closed his eyes, quieted his mind, and began to visualize how events might unfold. Planning on how to place the snake in Ms. Lawrence's office, he tried to think of problems that might occur. Dwaine thought it would be best if the snake were left in there for the entire weekend. *I'm sure nothing bad will happen. It will just scare Ms. Lawrence*, Dwaine had thought.

We will see about that.

Homicide Investigation

That evening, the front door was not pulled all the way closed. Mei, not thinking a thing about it, grabbed the doorknob and pushed the door open. Ready to tell Sampson the good news, she walked into the living room and saw the body of her lover lying on the carpet. His throat was slashed from side to side. His eyes, though open, were lifeless. She didn't notice it when she stepped on a partially-damp, bloody footprint. She didn't realize that she was holding her lover, crying, unable to put words together. What she did know was that he was gone. Her child would never know how caring his father was. Sampson saw the good in people. How would the child grow up not knowing the affection of such a loving father?

Then another thought came to her mind, *I am standing in a crime scene. This was going to be bad*. But she had to call 911.

◆ ◆ ◆

The police arrived and taped off the yard and house. An officer took down information from Mei. Investigator Bill Candler was called in. Paying particular attention to the victim's girlfriend, an Asian woman, he noticed that she had blood on her shoes and went immediately over to her.

"I am Investigator Candler. Tell me what happened," he said.

The crying stopped. "I came home a few minutes ago. I found Sampson lying on the carpet."

"And?" he said.

"And that's it," she looked up at the investigator.

"Did you touch him at all?" he asked.

"I found him like that, and I bent over to see if he was still alive."

"I..." she paused. "I picked his head up, and I held him."

"You are a reporter, right?" he asked.

"Yes," she said.

"You know you are not supposed to touch or move the body, right?"

"I, uh..." She felt so ashamed. She had criticized officers and other people for making such careless errors in the past.

"You do know that, right?" he asked again.

She nodded.

"Ms. Yun, do you know you have blood on your shoe?" He asked.

"I need a bag for the shoe," he called out to a subordinate. "Ma'am, we are going to need that shoe," he said. "And you are going to need to come with us."

When Mei Yun had been put into a squad car, Eddie Blair, a junior crime scene investigator, went over to Candler.

"Here is what we have so far," Eddie said. "Prints from the door knob, a blood-stained footprint on the carpet, her shoe with blood on it, and a piece of hair we found in the folds of the deceased's rolled up sleeve."

"Hurry and get it to the lab, and get a toxicology report." Bill looked over at a bottle that had been dropped on the floor. Walking into the kitchen, he saw the wine glass and an empty bottle of wine on the table.

"I doubt that a five-foot, two-inch woman could attack a six-foot man and win outright, but if he had been drinking that could change things."

Questions

Friday Morning did not start out pleasant. An impromptu meeting was called for the faculty. Ms. Lawrence said, "I am the bearer of horrible news." She paused for a moment to wipe a tear away.

"One of our own has passed. Sampson Damasks has been found dead in his home."

Many teachers were silent except for the teachers who broke down in tears.

She continued, "He was thirty-five. He had taught for ten years. He was a wonderful friend to both teachers and students, and I will surely miss him. The funeral will be next week. Try to go if you can. Also, we will be collecting money for a floral arrangement." She paused for a moment before moving on to the other matter. "This is Investigator Candler. He will be asking the faculty and staff some questions throughout the morning."

Investigator Candler step forward and said, "Ladies and gentlemen, these questions are very routine questions. We aren't certain what happened, but we will find out with your help."

Several teachers had questions and shouted.

Mrs. Howard asked, "How did he die?"

Mr. Hayes asked, "Was there foul-play involved?"

Investigator Candler said, "Folks, we will answer questions as soon as we get them and can make a determination."

◆ ◆ ◆

During first period, Dwaine was called to the front office. Ms. Lawrence and Investigator Candler were talking when he arrived.

"Mr. Mann, please have a seat." She paused as he took a seat and said, "This is Investigator Bill Candler," Ms. Lawrence said.

Investigator Candler cut in, "These are routine questions like I said." He looked at her and said, "Ms. Lawrence, could you give us some privacy?"

She promptly left.

"He was a good guy." Looking down, Dwaine shook his head and looked up. Then he continued, "Okay, so how can I help?"

"Well, we have talked to your colleagues about Sampson. A teacher said that you two had a disagreement after the faculty meeting."

"You think that I killed Sampson? He was a colleague and friend to me," Dwaine said.

"Well, I am not going that far, but we do want to rule you out," Investigator Candler said.

"We did get into an argument about a woman. He was upset that I had dated his girlfriend in college."

"A teacher said that you said, 'She's mine.'"

"Well, that's partially true. I said 'She *was* mine,'" He smiled when he lied. "We dated in college," Dwaine said.

"Plus, Ms. Lawrence is not a teacher, and she's the one who saw us arguing." Dwaine looked at him and tilted his head just a little. "I am not surprised that she would get the words mixed up and pin it on me. She has been on my case for a long time."

"So you're saying that..."

"I am saying that she would say anything and do anything to make me look bad," Dwaine said, then paused. "Hey man, check the cameras."

"We did. We saw that you two were into a scuffle."

"No, we didn't; it was a one-sided fight. He pushed me back against the wall. He nearly cracked my head."

"So you were not on good terms?"

"I was on good terms. He was the one who was upset at me," Dwaine said.

Writing on his pad, Investigator Candler said, "We will be in touch."

Dwaine stood up and walked away, saying, "Yeah, whatever you say."

Pet Deposit

Ms. Lawrence's office was relatively close to his room, so he figured it would be easy to put the snake in place. He would simply use a ladder to ascend to the ceiling. He would pull back a tile, crawl the distance to where her office was located, and deposit the snake. The problem was releasing the snake. Presently, the snake was now stored securely in the trunk of his car. He would pretend to work late, bide his time and wait for the right opportunity to make his move.

The kids were on track with their assignments and seemed to be in a particularly good mood. Dwaine sat at his desk while his last class worked and pondered how peaceful he felt. He wasn't nervous or sweating, and the pressure that often rose in his chest was absent. He actually felt good. A smile stretched across his face.

"Mr. Mann, I haven't seen you smile in a long time. It looks good on you," a student said out of nowhere.

"Thanks. You're a sweetheart," Dwaine said. "I have a big day ahead of me and an even bigger weekend."

"I bet you have a new woman," another student said.

"Something like that. But you know I don't talk about my personal life at school," he lied to quell the questioning.

A chorus of kids began chanting, "Woo hoo! Mr. Mann gonna get some."

The hour passed and students started scurrying about to go home. Busses had lined up outside of the academy in their designated positions, awaiting their throngs of passengers.

Soon, Dwaine thought. *Soon.*

The last of the students were ready to be released, so all he had to do now was wait for the teachers to leave. The janitorial staff would be the only ones remaining. Dwaine went over his notes mentally. *Make sure the janitors have cleaned Ms. Lawrence's office. Then you can drop the snake when everything is calm.*

After things quieted down and the janitors wrapped up their duties in his area, Dwaine quietly went to his car and retrieved the snake.

He opened the trunk, and then ensured the snake tube was securely covered by the thick cloth to muffle any rattling. He walked over to a bench by the sidewalk close to the door. He didn't want to scan his identity card to enter the building. Scans were recorded for security purposes, so using his card would mark that he had been there. He didn't have to wait long, as one of the janitors left. Dwaine jumped up and made his way to the door. "Can you hold the door please, Mr. Perez? My hands are a bit full."

Mr. Perez smiled, nodded his head in acknowledgement, and held the door wide open. He had come to the U.S. from El Salvador a few years earlier and didn't speak much English, although he understood the language fairly well.

"Gracias, Mr. Perez," Dwaine said as he hastened into the building.

There were children still milling about who had just finished basketball and cheerleading practices. No one paid Dwaine and his strange package any attention. *I might actually be able to keep my job after this,* he thought. Dwaine entered his classroom and sat his package on the floor. He retrieved a ladder from a back storeroom and proceeded to climb into the ceiling.

He crawled carefully placing his weight on the support beams. Once he was directly over Ms. Lawrence's office, he bit his lip. *I have to be careful; a bite could be deadly.* He pulled aside a tile, removed the lid to open the tube, and angled the tube slightly down toward the floor. The snake resisted at first. Then the rattling sound became louder. The snake's head peered out of the hole and turned back toward Dwaine. *Oh, shit!* he thought. The snake started to slither up the outside of the tube. He thought for sure the snake was going to bite him. Dwaine shook the tube vigorously. Finally, the snake fell to the office floor and immediately began slithering around, flicking its tongue.

"Okay, buddy, you are on your own," Dwaine said softly with an ear-to-ear smile. "Ms. Lawrence, enjoy your new pet."

Dwaine hung around in his classroom for a while longer to ensure that almost everybody had left the academy. He still had to get back to his car with the snake tube unnoticed. He made his way the short distance to the exit door and was about to get into his car when the Savage Voice spoke. *Step One is complete. It is time to raise the stakes on Ms. Lawrence. The snake isn't good enough. You have to show her who is in charge of the academy, and you must make more people pay.*

"Hey, wait a minute. I fulfilled my end of the bargain. I got back at her," Dwaine said to the Savage Voice.

Listen, Junior, you will do as I tell you. Understand? How about if I shoot some pain through your body? Just then his heart started to beat faster, and he felt an acute pain in his shoulder.

"Okay, stop," Dwaine cried out.

♦ ♦ ♦

Mei Yun's attorney arrived without delay after being notified of her situation.

"You have no grounds to hold my client," said Phil Taylor. "Do you honestly think she could kill him?" He took out the pictures of the deceased Sampson.

Phil continued, "Look at the angle of the knife cut on Sampson, someone had to be behind him to cut his neck," Phil Taylor said showing the picture of Sampson's cut. "Mei does not have the height or strength needed to kill Sampson."

"Well, she had blood on her shoe. She moved the body even if it was a little bit," Investigator Candler said.

"Well charge her with that instead of trying to pin her with murder."

"We will," Investigator Candler said.

"Speaking about blood on shoes, she doesn't own any boots and was wearing shoes half the size of the imprints. Since there were no other formal charges listed, and there were no other sets of prints found either," Taylor said as he paused, "I am leaving with my client."

Family Assault

It was Friday night and Rashad King and his family were returning from a night out. They had gone to a restaurant for an early dinner and then to watch a basketball game between business owners and staff in the main downtown park.

Rashad was a rather portly seventh grader. His belly lapped over his belt. He gripped an inhaler that he used to help him with his breathing. His cheeks hung over his jaw. Rashad spent most of his time studying hard. He particularly liked English literature because of all the drama and wit.

Because of his weight, he had always been shy, avoided peers, and clung to his family. His parents were grocery store owners, but he wanted to follow in the footsteps of his uncle, who was a civil rights attorney. His father and mother told him that there was no cause nobler than to stick up for those who have been hurt unjustly. He liked the idea of serving others.

Students often said things that were untrue about him, but he said nothing in response. The terms 'fatty' and 'fatso' hurt, but he ignored it. Because of his silence, other students tended to pick on him too.

Mr. Mann was his mentor and his friend. The man had told him that he had also once been the fat kid in class. "Some things never change," Mr. Mann had said. He had given Rashad extra attention and was helping him learn animation and graphic arts, specifically photo editing. More importantly, Mr. Mann helped him through the brutality and harshness he faced on a daily basis.

He had advised Rashad that when he felt stressed, he should think of the most peaceful memory he had experienced with his family and picture it in his head. The ability to feel genuine joy was part of the equation for becoming emotionally strong. For Rashad, his family was his strength. No matter how bad things were, someone was always there to offer him support.

"Visualize your happiness," Mr. Mann had told Rashad. This visualization technique had been drilled into Rashad to prepare him on how to deal with bullies and some of the stricter teachers. The techniques allowed him to keep his head and not succumb to fear. Rashad also learned to use the techniques to help prepare for tests and tough homework assignments. His grades had shot up, and now he was an honor student. His parents were extremely pleased with his academic performance and had thanked Mr. Mann for his selfless support.

Crime was rampant near the apartments where Rashad and his family lived. It hadn't always been that way, but the neighborhood was declining rapidly. Rashad had heard from other students that a gang, the Jags, had been recruiting at school. They had patches on their bandanas in the shape of Jaguars.

As Rashad's parents and sister were walking home from their SUV, a group of thugs ambushed them. Rashad had remained in the SUV. He had been searching for his book, and ended up seeing the assault through the window.

"Give me your money!" one of the Jags said.

Rashad recognized him. Terrell was a high school kid and knew him from the neighborhood. Terrell's long dreads hung down past his shoulders but were now tied back to keep them from getting in the way. He yelled again, "Give me the money, now!"

"No one carries cash anymore. It's too dangerous," Rashad's father said.

"Oh, you are a real clown," Terrell said.

"Here! Here's our debit card. Take it!" Rashad's father said. He didn't know what else to do.

"You motherfuckers get on the ground, now!" another Jag said. Rashad's family complied, slowly lowering themselves down to the sidewalk.

Rashad ducked to hide in the vehicle and dialed 911 on his cell phone. When the operator answered, he pleaded, "Pl... pl... please come to the apartments. My family is being attacked." His mind immediately recalled the time Mr. Mann had talked to him about focusing and controlling his emotions. Rashad stuttered horribly when he was upset, which had often interfered with school presentations and public speaking assignments. Mr. Mann had told him to count slowly, "One, two, three," he said. In this case, it was to be able to communicate with the police. *Find your center. Find your peace. Visualize that happiness* Rashad remembered Mr. Mann's words.

But he could not.

"How many people are attacking your family? Which apartments?" asked the man on the phone.

"Um, um, I'm afraid t... to look. Five, maybe s... s... six," he continued to stammer, speaking in a shaky voice. He tried to push the fear aside, but the intense emotion was too much.

"Keep calm, son," the dispatcher said in a calm voice.

"What is your location? Where are you exactly?"

"I, uh…" Rashad stumbled verbally.

"It's okay, just stay with me. I am setting up a ping on your phone," the dispatcher said.

"Wha… a ping?" A couple seconds went by. Rashad heard the dispatcher say off the phone, "Code 20 at the Winshaw apartments." He then said to Rashad, "There is a police car near you."

It took Rashad several moments to respond. "I'm at, at the apartments. Apartment 18, sir." He was in shock, and he could barely verbalize anything or think clearly. Ashamed, he lowered his head. He felt that he could not protect his family.

"Give me that phone!" came a demanding voice. Rashad rose up from his crouched position to see a Terrell standing by the door. The interior light showed an outline of a Jaguar was on his headband. Rashad held on to the phone, hoping to buy more time for the police, but the Jag snatched it away. He threw it down to the ground and stomped on it, shattering it to pieces.

"I've, I just…" Rashad spoke incoherently. He remembered the last time Terrell had shoved him against a wall.

He grabbed Rashad's shirt and pulled him out of the vehicle, closer to his family. Rashad was devastated at seeing his family kneeling in front of the other thugs with guns pointed at their heads.

"I just c… call…" He tried to form the words, but he stopped abruptly when he saw a Jag pistol-whip his mother.

"I called the police," Rashad finally spoke out.

Rashad wanted to distract the thugs from her and the rest of his family and stall for time.

Rage rose in Terrell's voice as he said, "Hit the bitch again."

The Jag was about to slap Rashad's mother again, but stopped when he saw blue lights coming around the corner.

"Po-po! Let's go," he said.

Terrell pulled Rashad closer and said, "We're going to remember this." He released Rashad with a violent push and slapped his father in the side of the head, then fled with the rest of the gang.

The girls were weeping uncontrollably. Rashad's mother gathered them up in a hug as they waited for the police to arrive. Rashad sat down on the curb and stared at the ground. After this, he doubted that he would ever be able to find his voice or stand up for anyone.

The Wedding

Saturday morning arrived in a flash. Victoria Lawrence struggled to crawl out of bed. A seething hangover prevented her eyes from opening fully. She was looking for her cell phone, frantic. Everything concerning the wedding, her agenda for the honeymoon, plane ticket information, hotel information, and more was stored on that phone. She searched everywhere—her house, her car—she even called the bar where they had partied the night before. *Where the hell did I leave it?* She was about to have a panic attack, so she sat down and calmed herself. The throbbing in her head lessened, and then it dawned on her. *Crap, I left it at the academy.*

Most of the teachers and administrators who were just married took a whole week off, but the future Mrs. Lawrence-Johnson was only taking Monday off for her honeymoon. *Aaron doesn't like it? Well, welcome to my world, baby.* The academy would go to hell if she wasn't there to keep it under control. Besides, she wouldn't want to miss the Black Heritage Celebration. "Damn, I know my phone is there!" she said.

Victoria used the house phone to call her sister and maid of honor, Diondra, and tell her she would meet her at the church. Her sister reported that the videographer had called to say that the deposit had not cleared. She added that Victoria's dress needed to be hemmed again. It was last minute, but necessary. Unfortunately, the seamstress would be late delivering it. Victoria had wanted everything to go smoothly, but the day was certainly not starting out well. She stood up, gained her composure, and confronted herself out loud, "Get a grip, Vicky. This is no time for a meltdown. You have to get ready and go to the academy for that damn phone!" Victoria scurried around to get dressed and stuffed makeup and other essentials into a bag. She ran out of the house, entered her car, and made her way to the academy.

Running, she entered the academy as fast as she could. She cursed, "Son of a bitch," when she hit her knee on a trashcan while turning the corner outside of her office. She offered other colorful curses as she dropped the keys to her office, fumbling to locate the right one. She finally slid the correct key into the lock and opened her office door.

She rushed inside and instantly froze in her tracks. Something felt out of place. She looked around and did not see it. But then she heard it. It sounded like a rattle. Shaking its tail, she felt impending doom. Coiled under the desk in the shadow was a snake. The noise became louder, and then it struck!

Moving her foot back, she felt the leathery snake as it just missed biting her leg. She backed up, then grabbed the door and almost fell. "Oh God!" she shrieked. She managed to get to the other side of the door, and then slipped. She was on the floor half-way out of her office, about eye-level with the snake. The snake recovered, and then it struck again. In slow motion, she could see the mouth open up to reveal two terrible fangs. Her hand on the doorknob, she pulled it for all she was worth, trying to close the door with one hand. With the door shut, she looked through the window in the door. The snake was stretched out right where her head had been just a moment ago.

No matter how hard Victoria tried, she could not quit shaking. That snake had almost killed her. A desperate thought flashed through her mind. *I will be lost without that phone! Will I have to cancel the wedding? I can't. This is my day, and everything is prepared. Oh my God! What am I going to do? I need my phone!* Victoria was in the hallway. It was four hours until the wedding. The snake was in her office. She had to get her phone, but she was not about to go in there. From the main office, she called Ms. Walker in a panic. Not only was Ms. Walker her boss, but the two of them had confided in each other from time to time. Victoria knew she would help.

Ms. Walker and Derek Griffin, her boyfriend, arrived within ten minutes.

Derek asked, "How did the snake get in there?"

"The hell if I know," Victoria said.

Ms. Walker snapped, "But there's no way it could have entered your office. What did you do, leave the door open? Did you leave food in there?"

She was starting to annoy Victoria. "You're treating me like a student." Apparently Ms. Walker didn't grasp the urgency of the situation or how irrelevant her comments were at the moment.

"What are you going to do about the wedding?"

"I'm getting married. It's too late to cancel. I have family here from Chicago." Victoria tried to keep from crying.

"Okay. Well, you better go to the church," Ms. Walker suggested. Victoria's hair was disheveled. Her leg was bleeding, as was her hand... not to mention the fact that she was an emotional wreck. And then, of course, there was her phone.

"But I need that phone!"

Ms. Walker attempted to calm her down. "I'll call animal control. We will get the phone."

Finally, Victoria conceded, "Okay, I guess I'll let you guys handle this."

"Don't even worry about it; you would do the same. Now go. We will be there with your phone," Ms. Walker said.

Victoria rushed to her car. For a moment, inside the car, she could not move. She could not catch her breath. Her heart was pounding as if it were going to explode. She had to drive, but she could not. She was scared. Her hands cupped over her face, and she started to sob.

Victoria looked up and saw a loud animal control truck stop two spots from her. The man ran toward the academy doors, carrying a hook and a thick sack. He stopped, turned around, and looked at her. *Why is he looking at me*? Her hair was a mess, and she had just stopped crying.

"Hey lady, you okay?" he asked.

Victoria came out of her delirium. Her life had almost been taken, and she was worried about a damn phone. She laughed hysterically.

"I don't know," she said, and drove off.

Breakdown

Victoria was numb from the frustration of the morning's events, and this wedding had consisted of nothing but problems. First, the hairdresser was overcharging her. She was sure of it. The cake was not ready, the flowers hadn't arrived yet, and her dress was still being hemmed.

Her three sisters met her at the door. Victoria was so upset that she couldn't speak. Soon after arriving, Ms. Walker and Derek had filled them in on the morning's events. On the plus side, they had been good enough to bring in her phone after animal control removed the snake.

"Damn, girl, you look like shit," Adrianna Lawrence said.

Victoria gave her a hurtful look. Finally, she said, "I was almost bitten by a snake. What do you expect?"

"How in the world did a snake get in your office?" Adrianna asked in bewilderment.

"It must have been cold and seeking shelter," her other sister, Shironda, offered, trying to diffuse the situation.

"The time for speculation is over. We must focus on the wedding," Diondra Lawrence said. She was the small but plump elder sister. She took control and began giving orders to those around her. "Victoria, there is a shower in the church annex. Hurry, the hairdresser is waiting."

The hairdresser was not in the best mood. She did not like waiting. Victoria explained the problem, but the woman still complained; getting the knots out of her hair was tedious.

"Quit complaining and get to work," Victoria snapped in a hateful tone.

"Mom's here," Shironda shouted as she scurried by on one of her errands. "The dress is here too!"

"Good," Victoria grunted. The bliss she had felt only a day earlier was completely gone. Her only concern was getting through the ceremony.

"How are you doing?" her mother asked when she entered. She was clearly worried. To see her daughter so shaken up, and on her wedding day, was disturbing. Very disturbing.

"I'll be better when this day is over."

"It is your day," her mother said, placing a reassuring hand on her shoulder.

"Thank you, mother," she said, still upset.

Trying to calm Victoria down, her mother said, "Darling, tell me about the first time you met Aaron."

A smile started to form on Victoria's face. "You know we met at church. He was a guest in our bible study group."

"What did you notice about him?"

"That man was dressed sharp."

"What else?"

"He had the best dimples," Victoria said. Her smile widen.

As the time for the ceremony neared, Victoria's joy began to return. She was focused on the moment and, finally, after a terrible morning, she was happy. She got into position outside the chapel, and her uncle stood by her side. Her father had died a dozen years earlier from a massive heart attack. Since there were no brothers in the family, Victoria had asked her uncle, Brady, to give her away.

The music began playing and the door opened wide. Aaron was standing at the front of the chapel, smiling broadly. *He is so handsome,* Victoria thought. *This is my day, my day to cherish.*

When the music started, Victoria began the slow, deliberate walk down the aisle with her uncle. Her stomach began to churn. As she watched Aaron standing in the distance in his light gray suit, she wondered if she would be a good wife. The thought sent pangs of doubt through her. *So much of my time is wrapped up in school work. Will I be able to give Aaron my best? God, I don't know if I can do this!*

The problems of the day returned to haunt her. They filed through her now tormented mind. Her brow sank as she thought about how she wanted to verify her honeymoon reservations one last time, but had forgotten due to the... She paused a brief moment.

Victoria began to tremble. Her uncle felt it and clutched her hand a bit tighter. She felt her face twitch. She wanted to cry. *This is my day.* She repeated the thought to herself over and over again, trying to ease her troubled mind.

The walk down the aisle seemed to take forever. The pair finally approached Aaron and the preacher. Victoria was sweating profusely now. She turned her eyes to Aaron for comfort and saw something else. The body language and facial expression of her love, her fiancé, and her soon-to-be husband spoke volumes. It looked like regret. He looked like he didn't want this. She shook.

Victoria was losing her composure. She felt suffocated, like the walls of the church were closing in on her and everyone there, pushing the guests closer to her. She felt surrounded and embraced by it, but it wasn't a pleasant embrace. No, it was like that of an anaconda... choking the happiness from her soul. *The snake. I can't get that snake out of my mind. How the hell did it get in there? What if there are more? Maybe it has a nest.*

Victoria and her uncle stopped at the end of the aisle.

The preacher began, "We gather together on this day..."

His words faded away as fear and panic gripped Victoria's mind. She looked around at the crowd of family, friends, and acquaintances that filled the church. She saw Ms. Walker fanning herself as if feeling Victoria's anxiety.

Her attention returned to the preacher when she heard him speak her name. "Do you, Victoria Lawrence, take Aaron Johnson to have and to hold?"

"For better or for worse? For richer or poorer? In sickness and in health?"

"Until death..."

I almost died today.

"Will you Victoria..."

That snake almost killed me! Oh my God. Her mind began torturing her again with thoughts of her busy schedule, the major life changes she would have to make, whether or not she could even be a good wife deserving of Aaron's love.

Victoria heard one of the women behind her say, "Look at her. She looks like she is having a nervous breakdown."

I feel so helpless and weak. Will I ever be the strong, confident woman Aaron fell in love with again? Or will I be broken? A burden?

She saw Aaron's sour facial expression. She was shaking. Victoria mistook the look of concern with disgust. *He looks disgusted with me.*

She stopped and looked down, putting her hand to her mouth.

I can't do this, Victoria thought.

She still could not stop shaking. *I can't do this.* Victoria's thoughts verbalized into a terrified scream, "I can't do this!" She looked at Aaron with wide, startled eyes and then turned and ran back down the aisle. She was weeping uncontrollably now, holding her floor-length dress up as she ran. She burst through the doors and out of sight.

Chapter Six

Left Out in the Cold

It was a particularly frosty Monday morning. A cold front had moved through the night before, leaving a harsh chill in the air. Dwaine arrived early. He parked near the door close to his classroom and exited the car, pulling a duffle bag from the passenger seat. Several students were huddled together outside the door waiting to be let in. It was the academy's policy not to allow students in until 7:30 a.m. sharp, after the teachers had arrived and could provide supervision.

It was only 6:50 a.m., but some students had either been dropped off early by working parents or had been forced to walk to the academy. They normally liked to gather and chat before school started, but this morning was particularly cold and almost unbearable. The five students stood at the door, shivering. A few were rubbing their hands together. The others had stuffed their hands in pockets to keep them warm. One very thin girl was freezing, unable to keep from shivering violently.

As Dwaine approached the door, the students greeted him and asked to be let inside the academy. He knew the policy, and he knew he would get bitched out by Ms. Lawrence if he let the kids in. He could normally resist the pitiful requests of students, but poor Rachel looked like she might actually develop hypothermia. He looked around. *This is ridiculous!*

Dwaine shook his head in disgust. *That bossy bitch is on her honeymoon anyway,* he thought. "Come on, kids. Let's go inside." The students managed to grin a little. "Just promise me one thing," he said as he slid his ID card through the security lock.

"Anything, Mr. Mann," the kids said in unison, except for Rachel whose teeth were chattering, her lips blue.

"You all go straight to your lockers. Stay there until the homeroom bell rings. And stay out of trouble." He pivoted around to ensure that he had made eye contact with each student, to show he was serious. Then he smiled and opened the door wide, and they all shuffled in.

The kids turned down the hallway leading to their lockers while Dwaine took long strides towards his classroom. He looked left and then right to see if anyone was around. His eyes peered from between his coat collar—which he had flipped up to keep the wind off his neck—and the bill of his ball cap. It was the same ball cap that had thrown Ms. Lawrence into a frenzy when they had first met. He hadn't worn it to the academy in a long time, but this was a special occasion. She wasn't here.

Dwaine unlocked his classroom door, entered, and shut it behind him. He stopped to peer outside again to check if anyone was around. He was in a good mood, even whistling. He'd had a successful weekend hacking into the academy's network, downloading schematics onto a disk, and having them printed just in case he needed them. But his good mood suddenly turned a little apprehensive. He didn't see anyone, but he could hear the laughter of the students he'd let in echoing through the hall. *Those urchins are gonna get me in trouble.*

Dwaine took off his coat and hat and hung them on the wall. He placed the duffle bag on his desk. It contained three remote control cars, each with a package of explosives duct taped to the top. Also in the bag were a blueprint tube, a remote, three disks, and a transmitter. Arming the cars would have to wait; he took one of the disks and synced his laptop to the cars and the remote to the cars. He could check the location of the three cars with the laptop and detonate with either device. Dwaine produced a large, wicked smile. *After this prank, no one will want to send their child here.* Putting everything up, he zipped up the bag, stowed it in the large bottom drawer of his desk, and engaged the lock.

Basil Scion

Hearing the kids down the hall, he decided he'd take a walk towards Ms. Lawrence's office and check on the kids. He hoped those kids weren't causing mischief.

Walking down the hall he thought, *I wonder what is going on with the snake.*

Seeing Mr. Sellars, he said, "Good morning, Mr. Sellars. How are you today?"

"Honestly, I'm a bit ticked off, Mr. Mann," the janitor replied.

"What's the matter?"

"Ms. Walker called me in. I had to come in Saturday to clean up Ms. Lawrence's office."

Dwaine's eyes widened with disappointment. *Did he almost get bit? Did Ms. Lawrence not have to deal with the snake?*

Dwaine feigned confusion. "Why?"

Of course, he already knew the answer, but he was forced to play the schmuck. It would be fun hearing the details from someone else.

"A snake somehow made its way into her office. It nearly got Ms. Lawrence. It made quite a mess, too. It left droppings." Mr. Sellars shook his head.

Thoughts of revenge and the resulting satisfaction raced through his mind. *Ha!* He continued his inquiry. "On Saturday?" Dwaine paused, but did not give enough thought about what to say. "Oh... that's terrible"

Dwaine said, "Thanks for your hard work. I've gotta go check on the kids that I let in the academy."

Dwaine turned down a hall that led past the academy's trophy case and Ms. Lawrence's office. "She was here!" He laughed to himself. *This is great! It couldn't have worked out any better. I bet that ol' bitch had the scare of her life.*

He could see the kids huddled together on the floor in front of the lockers, talking and laughing. He walked up to them to chat about their weekends. He hadn't been there but a few minutes when he heard a booming female voice behind him.

"Mr. Mann! What are those kids doing in the school?"

He swung around. *Oh God, it's Ms. Lawrence.* "They were outside freezing, so I let them in. Before you get all worked up, I am standing here with them."

She looked like she had lost all joy in life. "Just don't do it again... okay?" She shut the door.

"Wow," one of the boys said, "She didn't even chew you out!"

Dwaine looked at the group. "Yeah. Weird, huh?"

He turned away from the kids, adding a quick, "See ya later," and made his way to Ms. Lawrence's office. He tapped on the door a few times, then poked his head in. "Everything okay? I thought you were sup-posed to be on your honeymoon today."

Ms. Lawrence was standing behind her desk, texting away. She didn't look up.

Dwaine heard her say as she texted, "No, I don't want to talk about it, Aaron."

She looked up, like she was expecting to see a ghost. The sudden interruption seemed to trigger her. She started shaking. Dwaine noticed a tear rolling down her face. He almost felt sorry for her... almost.

"Are you okay?" Dwaine asked.

Ms. Lawrence came around like she was going to attack him, but simply screamed, "Get out! Get out now!"

Her voice was forceful, but her body language showed nothing but weakness, total defeat.

He went back to the classroom. Once inside his classroom, Dwaine sat a bag of chips on his desk, unlocked the bottom drawer, and re-trieved the duffle bag. *I shouldn't do this*, he thought. His shoulder felt numb.

But you will. You are just going to scare some folks, the Savage Voice spoke.

No violence, okay? Dwaine thought back.

He grabbed the bag of chips and munched on a few as he made his way to the back storeroom. He retrieved the ladder and positioned it near where he'd climbed up with the snake. He climbed up the ladder, pulled a screwdriver out of his back pocket, and removed a panel for an air duct exposing the inside. Next, he placed one of the remote-controlled cars facing one direction and the two others facing the opposite direction. He flipped a switch on each car and checked to make sure the little green light came on. He replaced the panel and the ceiling tile, and then returned the ladder to the storeroom.

He sat down at his desk, and turned on his laptop. He grinned at how easy it was. He gently pushed in the disk. A list of programs popped up on the screen, and Dwaine selected the one that showed a lay out of the school. On screen, he could see the location of the cars; he used the remotes to maneuver all three cars in the ducts. He placed one by the chorus room, another over the lunch room, and the last car in the gym.

As Dwaine was making a beeline for the door and stepping outside of the classroom, he heard that oh-so-familiar voice coming from down the hall. "Mr. Mann, I want a word with you." It was Ms. Lawrence.

"I really need to be going," he said, loud enough for her to hear him.

She just kept walking without saying a word until she was standing right in front of him, too closely. "Don't you think I forgot about those kids you let into the academy this morning. I'm just letting that one slide because of tomorrow's celebration, and because I had a rough weekend. I really did not want to deal with you today."

"Speaking of that... What happened this weekend? Why aren't you on your honeymoon today?"

"Because, Mr. Mann, in case you haven't heard—and everyone has—I was almost bitten by a snake in my office." She looked down. Then she looked up, as if something had just occurred to her. "You wouldn't know anything about that, would you?"

He froze. *How did she know?*

The Savage Voice spoke in his head. *Shut up. No one has arrested you yet.*

She paused, looking at Dwaine. "Anyway, the wedding was a complete disaster and... and..." Ms. Lawrence turned away from Dwaine. She couldn't quite grab hold of her emotions in time. Her eyes welled up with tears, but she refused to let them go. She tried to compose herself, wiped her eyes with one hand, and turned back to face Dwaine. "I didn't go through with it," she said in a shaky voice.

"You didn't get married?" Dwaine asked.

"No, I did not get married. Now, you had better be on your best behavior tomorrow. I don't want to have to deal with any disrespect from you." She pretended to act and sound like the authority figure that her job required her to be, but her voice... It just wasn't the same. It spewed weakness, and this realization did not escape Dwaine.

Holy shit. I broke the bitch. I actually broke her.

"There will be too many important people there and too many folks who will expect to enjoy the celebration. Do you understand?" She looked up and glared into his eyes without so much as a blink as she tapped her foot nervously.

"You won't hear a peep out of me."

"And what the hell are you doing wearing that damn hat? I thought we had an understanding that you would not wear it in the academy."

Dwaine felt the blood rise to his face. He wanted to have it out with her right then and there. Just as he was about to open his mouth, his Savage Voice offered some advice. *Don't do it! Stay focused! She will get hers tomorrow.*

Dwaine thought back against the Savage Voice. *But I just broke her.*

She needs to learn who is in charge and to do that we need a crowd. She cracked at her wedding now we will break her in front of the school, the Savage Voice retorted.

Dwaine took a deep breath and said, "I apologize. I ran out of the house in a hurry this morning and just grabbed something to keep my head warm. I didn't even realize it was that hat until after I was already here. I didn't mean to shake you up, Ms. Lawrence. It won't happen again." He feigned humility. Despite his obedient act, he was beaming with pride.

"It better not!" She walked away from Dwaine, and at that point it was obvious to him that she was an emotional wreck and didn't feel like she could do anything about him.

More Questions

Monday evening, there was a knock on Dwaine's door at home. He woke up from a nap and opened it to find Investigator Candler looking impatient.

"What do you want?" Dwaine asked.

"We want you to come to the station," Investigator Candler said without blinking.

"Why can't I answer your questions here?" Dwaine asked.

"We just need to clear something up."

"Look, I've already given you my story about Sampson."

"It will only take a few minutes, unless that is you have something to hide," Investigator Candler said.

"Let me get my coat."

At the station, Dwaine was led to a small room with window.

Investigator Candler said, "In our investigation, we found one of your hairs caught in the folds of Sampson's rolled-up sleeve."

"I think I know how that got there," Dwaine said. Oddly enough, the Savage Voice was not making any snide comments in his head.

"We also found a bloody imprint of boot soles on the carpet. Where were you Thursday evening?"

"I was home." Thinking about his hair, he added, "My hair was cut the other day." Dwaine laughed. "At the faculty meeting, Mr. Hayes was making fun of me, said something about me shedding more than his dog." He tried to hide his embarrassment. "When Sampson started a fight with me, he pushed me into a wall. I guess that's when a hair must have dropped into his sleeve."

"What size boots do you wear?" Eddie Blair asked.

"Size ten, I think," Dwaine said. "Look, I want to help out."

Eddie faced Investigator Candler and said in a low voice, "The boot's imprints came out to be a size twelve."

Investigator Candler said, "Do you mind if we take a look at your shoes for a moment?"

"Uh, Okay." Dwaine hesitated, then pulled off the shoes and handed it to him.

Looking inside the dress shoe, they saw the number ten.

Investigator Candler said, "That takes care of the boot issue." He paused, "Now all we need to do is clear up the issue of the hair. We are going to hold you for a little bit longer until we get this settled."

Moving Pieces into Place

Tuesday morning Dwaine awoke twenty minutes before his alarm was set to go off. Investigator Candler and Blair released him late last night after they confirmed with Mr. Hayes about the hair. Dwaine was humiliated for relying on someone else, in this case Mr. Hayes, for his freedom.

But now he had a job to do. He remembered that the Black Heritage Celebration was today, and this time he wanted to attend. He pondered for a moment how his new Savage Voice had set him free from the nagging, often debilitating, White Guilt Voice. In some ways, the Savage Voice made him feel whole, as if he were in charge of his life again.

He grabbed a bagel from a basket on the kitchen table and a brown paper bag he had prepared the night before. He put his coat on and rushed out the door. It was early, so traffic was light. He made it to the academy in a mere ten minutes, parking in his usual spot at the door closest to his classroom. The morning was cold, but not nearly as bitter as the day before. He mused that there were no kids waiting at the door, but once he walked into the academy, he realized various teachers and personnel were already there getting ready for the day's event.

Several cafeteria workers rushed by him on their way to the kitchen as he quickly unlocked his classroom door and slipped inside.

Dwaine looked at his watch. He would have time to set up, undisturbed, after the kids went to the gym. He took out the disk and plugged it into his laptop. He turned the computer on, and he took a quick look to see that his cars were in the positions. He had hacked into the video loop that ran throughout the entire academy. He could now call up any of the various cameras around the school to see what was going on in each room.

He wanted to test out the cameras, so he honed in on the kitchen. He knew for a fact that people were already there. The screen flickered and an image appeared. Standing in the middle of the kitchen was Mrs. Waddell, head of the kitchen staff. She was wearing her county uniform. It was gray on white, and made her look like a prison guard.

Dwaine was amused at the way Mrs. Waddell just stood there barking orders. It was obvious that she got off on a power trip, he thought.

He hastily pulled up the control panel and made another couple of selections and adjustments.

She raised a school radio to her mouth. Mrs. Waddell's voice came through his computer speaker, "...ss Ma'am. We are getting things prepared on our end. First we'll feed the breakfast crowd, and then we'll get things ready for lunch."

Another voice came through once Mrs. Waddell stopped talking. "Great, I'll be there in a few minutes." It was Ms. Lawrence.

Many of the students regularly ate breakfast at academy, which was mandated by the state. The staff also had to have an extra lunch prepared for the guests at the celebration.

Dwaine continued watching the hustle and bustle and the flailing of Mrs. Waddell's arms. He laughed about how easy it had been to hack into the video and radio transmissions. *Piece of cake,* he thought. Having eyes and ears all over the academy would help him pull off his plan of revenge effortlessly. His computer program, on a removable disk, would completely jam all phone and radio transmissions within the academy, but he would wait to use that later.

He continued watching the cafeteria crew frantically scrambling under the stern direction of Mrs. Waddell. An employee approached her and told her that one of the ovens wasn't working. Mrs. Waddell began waving her arms frantically. She snatched the radio. With a crackle of static emitted from the radio, she called one of the janitors to see if they could help.

The students made their way down the hall and were herded to the cafeteria tables.

Mrs. Waddell's voice rang out over a microphone. "We have a problem with some of the cafeteria equipment, so we cannot serve breakfast right now. Sit in your designated seats."

The Savage Voice said *I have an idea. Send the Superintendent, his staff, and some parents an email about the ovens.*

Thirty minutes had passed. Students became exceedingly restless, and the teachers were trying to calm them down. Cafeteria staff rushed into the main area armed with trays of cold snacks that had been reserved for later use, but this was an emergency. If the kids didn't get something to eat to fill their idle time, things could veer out of control quickly.

Dwaine used his laptop and began scanning through the surveillance camera images. As he pulled up the parking lot cameras, he saw Mr. Nicholas's SUV pull into the parking lot.

The radio lit up with Ms. Lawrence's voice. "The Superintendent is here! And he's early! Get to your stations, and see to it that things remain in order."

Dwaine had to give the guy credit. While he was an obnoxious ass, Mr. Nicholas was a problem solver who kept the academy and county out of trouble. The only issue Dwaine knew of was that there were vicious rumors that the man's son was heavily involved in drugs.

The Superintendent of Picks County marched into the academy, surrounded by his entourage of staff. Mr. Nicholas was former military, so he was always prompt and sharply dressed.

Because of the email about the ovens, he had chosen to arrive early to help direct the activities of the staff. This was an important day not only for Mount Reese but also for the entire county.

Mr. Nicholas went directly to the academy's office without saying a word. Ms. Lawrence met him at the door. "Good morning, Mr. Nicholas."

"Is it?" he asked, almost interrupting her. "Where is Ms. Walker? She should be here organizing everyone."

"She will be here soon. I think she was in the cafeteria earlier."

"Do you know how important this day is for us all, Ms. Lawrence? If anything goes wrong, people could lose their jobs. And the ones not performing up to par will be history." The threat was painfully obvious.

Ms. Walker came up behind Ms. Lawrence, clearly distressed. She tried to hide her frustration. "We are doing everything possible to fix the ovens. We have called maintenance."

"This is your school, your kitchen, your people. Fix it now!" Mr. Nicholas roared. He paused a moment to let his orders sink in and then barked, "Why are you here? Get going!"

Ms. Lawrence rushed down to the cafeteria kitchen. On her way, Dwaine heard her scold Mrs. Waddell over the radio. "You'd better have things under control, or heads will roll!"

Dwaine knew that most people did not intimidate Ms. Lawrence, but from the sound of things Mr. Nicholas was doing a good job of it.

Drug Bust

With the celebration coming up, the janitors had been called to move chairs into the gym. Dwaine used this opportunity to slip into the janitors' office and make a call from the school phone. He had a smart phone, but he wanted the number to show up from the facility.

He dialed the Statesboro Police Department.

"What is the nature of the emergency?" the police dispatch responded.

"Hello, yes, I'm, ah, I'm calling to report that I've seen students selling drugs at Mount Reese. I'm a janitor here," Dwaine said with a Latin accent.

The lie was partially true. He knew that the Jags and other kids sold cocaine and marijuana in the hallways. The police wouldn't doubt his story. As a matter of fact, it had been a while since the police had conducted a contraband search at the academy, so he knew they would use this opportunity to do so.

"Have you informed the principal, sir?" asked the dispatcher.

"I have tried, but she is so busy; she just ignores me."

"Okay, we will send someone over."

Dwaine hung up the phone and started to leave the janitor's office. He opened the door and stood face to face with Mr. Sellars.

"What are ya doing in our office, Mr. Mann?" he asked suspiciously.

Dwaine darted his eyes back and forth, searching for an excuse. "Aw, dang, you know... I was looking for something to clean the computer keyboards. I looked for a janitor, but you all seemed tied up with setting up for the festivities," Dwaine lied. The Savage Voice filled his mind. *He knows what you're up to.*

"You know you aren't supposed to be in our office," Mr. Sellars said matter-of-factly.

"Hey, ya'll come into our classrooms all the time," Dwaine said, trying to be funny to avert suspicion, but it wasn't working. An image popped into his head of driving a screwdriver into the side of Mr. Sellar's head. The Savage Voice spoke again. *You need to get rid of this guy. He could ruin everything.* "Look, I'm sorry. One of those kids spilled powdered sugar next to one of my computers, and it has caked up the ventilation intake. You know how stingy the academy is about resupplying equipment. I just wanted to get it fixed ASAP."

"Aw right, don't let it happen again. I know you're a good guy, Mr. Mann."

"Hey, I owe you one."

"You sure do. I want a hot woman and a cold beer," Sellars said with an ear-to-ear grin.

"The cold beer I can help you with. The hot woman? Well, you're on your own with that one." Both Dwaine and Mr. Sellars laughed. Dwaine left as quickly as possible. He made his way down the hallway and into his empty classroom. He flipped open his computer and pulled up the control panel. The time for action was drawing near.

◆ ◆ ◆

The police attempted to call Ms. Walker. If there was to be a contraband check or the arrival of an undercover police officer to the academy, the principal was to be notified. However, Ms. Walker was not at her desk, so she did not get the message.

A little later, it came as a big shock to Ms. Lawrence when Officer London strolled into the cafeteria. He was met there by Officer Bates. Superintendent Nicholas was standing next to her.

Officer London, who was holding the leash of a German Shepherd, said, "Ms. Lawrence, we've had a report by one of the janitors of drugs being sold on school property."

Officer Bates was talking with Ms. Lawrence. She was standing in front of the dog, giving it a customary pat on the head. But the dog became fidgety. London gave the dog a bit more leash to see what was causing him to react. The dog began lunging toward the cafeteria doors. Both officers scanned the area to determine a potential suspect. Ms. Walker had just entered the cafeteria to see what all the commotion was about, but she froze when Ms. Lawrence moved out of the way of the dog's pawing.

"Seek!" Officer London commanded, while at the same time giving the leash to the dog a bit more slack, so it could find the drugs. The dog went straight to Ms. Walker and began whining and pawing at the small clutch purse she was carrying.

"Whoa! Officer London, what's going on?" Officer Bates asked.

"Justice has picked up a scent," he replied.

Officer Bates walked over to face Ms. Walker. Just as he did, Officer Lemez entered through the cafeteria doors behind her. Ms. Walker held on to her purse for dear life, her eyes wide with fear. The dog pawed excitedly at it.

Officer Bates could not believe what was happening. He took the purse and opened it, casting a serious glare at Ms. Walker in the process. "Do you mind if we take a look?" he asked as a matter of duty. He began removing items from the purse. He opened her wallet and looked at her ID. He passed the wallet to Officer London and reached in again. This time he pulled out a vial of cocaine.

Officer Bates gave a sigh and said with regret, "Hands behind your back, please, and lock your thumbs together. You're under arrest for possession of a controlled and dangerous substance." While he was applying the handcuffs, Offer Bates said, "Mr. Nicholas, it's a shame you had to be here to see this." There was no response. Officer Bates looked around at the other officers and asked, "Where is Mr. Nicholas? He was just here a minute ago."

Still holding Ms. Walker's arm, Officer Bates depressed the button on his radio attached to his shoulder and requested dispatch to send over another unit. The other officers began questioning if anyone had seen Mr. Nicholas leave. One of the kitchen staff said that he left down the hall.

One child laughed and said, "The po-po is going to get Mr. Nicholas."

Dwaine shifted in his seat as he watched the episode unfold from the cafeteria cameras. He heard the police calls over the radio as they searched for Mr. Nicholas. He decided it was time to contact the media. Mei Yun's station was close to the school. The town was not that big. He hurriedly typed an email and, with a click of the mouse, he sent it to Mei. The text said, 'Drug Bust Involving the Principal.'

A call went across the police radios, "Mr. Nicholas is going to the parking lot." After a minute, Officer London had Mr. Nicholas pinned in his SUV. The dog was leaping and barking at the scent of drugs.

Justice was lunging towards the back of the SUV. Noticing the trained behavior, Officer London gave the familiar command, "Seek!" Officer London gave him some slack; the dog went straight to the back, sniffed wildly, and put a paw on the bumper. Approaching the driver's side, he said, "Sir, I am going to need you to step out of the car. I'm sure there is a misunderstanding," he said.

After a tense ten seconds went by, Mr. Nicholas finally conceded and opened the door.

As he made his way around to the back of the SUV with Officer London, a media van pulled into the parking lot with screeching tires. "Great. How did they get wind of this so quick?" Officer London mumbled to himself. The van stopped just short of the action as Officer Lemez rushed to prevent it from coming any closer. Mei Yun and a hipster-look-ing cameraman jumped from the van. The man was turning on a video camera as she hastened him along.

"Please open the trunk, Mr. Nicholas," Officer London said. At that moment, Officer Bates arrived with the handcuffed Ms. Walker in tow.

The media had no intention of missing the "live events" as they unfolded. Other news station vans started to pull in to the parking lot. The cameras went live when Mr. Nicholas opened the trunk, and Mei Yun reported front and center. The onslaught of the reporter and the photos being taken caused Mr. Nicholas to wince.

Officer Martin pulled into the parking lot just behind the news vans. Getting out he said, "Please stand back and let us conduct this investigation,"

Mr. Nicholas was sweating profusely. When the trunk opened, there were several pounds of marijuana in it. With video rolling and cameras flashing, Mr. Nicholas adjusted his tie in a vain attempt to look more authoritative and dignified.

Mei Yun and her cameraman had their attention turned to the trunk of the SUV. With the scene in the background, Mei looked into the camera and began her report. "The investigation is just now starting. We are now seeing an inspection of Superintendent Nicholas's vehicle. It appears that the police dog has allegedly detected drugs in the back of the SUV." She paused, moving her waving hair out of her eyes as the wind blew. "We at VETT NEWS of Statesboro can only wonder why the drugs are in his SUV."

Mr. Nicholas froze. After a moment, he began patting down his forehead with a handkerchief. He said, "These drugs are not mine. I don't know why they are there."

After securing Ms. Walker in a squad car, Officer Bates was able to focus on the Superintendent. "Wow, what a haul," he told Officer London. "This is really going to mess things up for the schools," he said, shaking his head at the situation.

"Mr. Nicholas, please place your hands behind your back," Officer Bates said. The camera crews were focused on the arrest.

"I want my attorney," Mr. Nicholas replied in a gruff voice.

"I'm sure you do. You can call from the police department. Please come with me." Officer Bates led Mr. Nicholas towards another police car and read him his rights.

Dwaine peered at his laptop screen that was capturing the big arrest from a parking lot surveillance camera. In a couple of hours, news sites would broadcast the story.

In the office, Ms. Lawrence ordered the academy on lockdown due to the arrests. Teachers were advised to keep students where they were until further notice. Both she and the police wanted to avoid hundreds of curious kids getting in the way or taking advantage of such a sensitive event.

Dwaine continued to watch the chaos unfold on his laptop. Although his main target was Ms. Lawrence, the added prize of sticking it to that obnoxious Superintendent and an administrator like Ms. Walker was a sweet victory. A broad smile crossed his face, produced by a warm sensation that surged through his body. The Savage Voice blurted in Dwaine's mind, *We have to get Ms. Lawrence now.*

With the students on lockdown, the police started their search of the school. Twelve hundred students were enrolled at Mount Reese Academy; the complete search would take some time. It was going to be a long day especially with the celebration after lunch.

As the police made their way into the academy, the supervising teacher in each room was instructed to have the students exit and line up in the hallway against the walls. Officer London and Justice led the way followed by Officer Martin and Officer Bates, walking in a slow procession down the hall. They started at the exit and walked toward the center of the school to prevent any students who might have drugs from trying to slip out of the exit. Dwaine continued to monitor the situation, switching cameras as the officers moved about the academy.

Settle a Score

Mickey made his way to the academy through a path in the trees near the playground. He had been shamed and humiliated. Now, he had a score to settle. The thought of sticking it to two teachers sent a thrill of exhilaration coursing through his body. His grip tightened on the assault rifle he was carrying.

Mickey's eyes squinted as he continued his approach, his mind whirling in a blaze of thoughts. Mickey's math teacher, Mr. Pence, had given him a failing grade on an important test. Mickey had already been struggling in school, especially in math. He knew that if he failed math class then he might fail seventh grade. Mickey hated school and couldn't bear the thought of doing another year. *Maybe I should just drop out.* He hesitated. *I can't.* It really pissed him off that he had nowhere to go. He'd heard that he had to be sixteen to drop out of school. He felt like a door was shutting on his life.

And yet another door had slammed shut on him. The ultimate insult and the ultimate betrayal was that Sylvia Willis would not give him the time of day. She was an attractive teacher in her late twenties that Mickey had an obsessive crush on. Her long black hair was as smooth as silk and was never out of place. Her skin was a clear, without any blemish. She was an ebony goddess who deserved to be worshiped. Before she'd gotten pregnant, Mickey had thought she was svelte, always wearing the most beautiful dresses he had ever seen. And he loved the smile she wore every day of the week.

She, unlike many teachers, always had a kind word for the students. The one day Mickey had dressed sharp, she had complimented him.

Mickey had overheard her once, talking to another teacher about who the father of her baby was and how he had left when he'd found out she was pregnant. Mickey, being the gentleman that he was, had felt it was his responsibility to take care of Sylvia and her baby. He thought he was a man, after all, so he knew better than everyone. He had dressed up in his best suit and tie, and spent the small amount of money that he had saved on a bouquet of roses.

When he'd brought them to Sylvia's house, Mickey thought that she seemed appreciative, at first.

"I am sorry Mickey. You know that I cannot accept the flowers. I don't date students."

Mickey had felt a kick to the gut. He was being rejected. "What's wrong? Don't you like the flowers?" he'd asked.

"The flowers… are not the problem. You are a boy. A boy trying to be a man. I've have to go now."

Mickey could not understand why she'd been resisting. He'd grabbed her arm and said, "I want to take care of you!"

After she smacked his hand away, he had rushed her and fell on top of her. Seeing his prize was trying to escape, Mickey had tried to pin her down. He'd felt severe pain as a hand squeezed his testicles. She'd gotten away then slamming the door in his face. Banging on it, he had cried out to her. Only minutes had passed when the police showed up. After a brief struggle, they took Mickey away.

As he was being dragged away in handcuffs, Mickey had thought to himself, *doesn't she love me? How could she do this to me?* In a manner of moments, he'd gone from a hopeful love with the promise of a beautiful life with Sylvia to a wounded, dejected soul.

After he was released from juvy, he'd sat on the curb brooding over his rotten life. He'd wanted to leave home. While pondering his situation, a Jag walked up and began talking to him. Mickey had desperately needed someone to talk to, and the Jags had given him a listening ear.

Mickey had been friends with some of the Jags in the past, and now this Jag saw him as a good prospect. It was time to take him to the next level. They'd told him that if he would join them, they'd take care of him and make sure anyone who hurt him would pay. That promise had sounded really good to Mickey. He'd brightened up at the prospect of being a part of a group that seemed to actually care for him.

The Jags invited him to party at their clubhouse that night. The members had seemed like a bunch of brothers around each other… a family. He'd had his first taste of liquor that night. He'd smoked his first joint. One of the guys had introduced him to a girl, saying that if he joined he could party with the girls every weekend. He told them that he wanted in the gang.

The next night, they'd met again at the clubhouse. Mickey had known something was up when four boys surrounded him.

His friend, one of the four, had said quietly, "Cover your head."

Carmichael Jones, the Jag leader, was standing in front of them with a solemn look on his face. He'd given a nod, and suddenly Mickey could only feel pain from multiple punches. A punch had hit him in the side. He'd turned around to face the attacker and caught a fist smashing into his jaw. Immediately, he'd raised his hands to cover his face, which had left his ribs unprotected and two fists from different sides caught them.

"Ten," someone had called out. It had sounded like Carmichael.

He'd fallen to the floor, where the punches were replaced by kicks. He had cried out. No one was listening to his pleas to stop.

"Twenty," Carmichael had called out. "Don't cut him any slack."

The four assailants had kept kicking him in the ribs and pounding his face.

"Please stop, please," Mickey had kept saying, protecting his head.

A boy had found his stomach exposed and drove a foot into it. Mickey could swear that he had felt the pain all the way to his back.

"Thirty! Hell yea, get that man up!"

Bloody and bruised, Mickey had to be helped up.

Carmichael had stepped up and given him hug. "Welcome, brother."

Mickey had felt accepted. Carmichael had said that now that he was a brother, they would watch his back and protect him, and he them.

Although the Jags hadn't specifically called on Mickey to shoot his teachers, they had thought Ms. Willis and Mr. Pence both needed to learn a lesson. And as a new member, Mickey wanted to show his new family that their acceptance of him had not been in vain. He wanted to get revenge.

The celebration was coming up. What better way for Mickey to show how tough he was than to make an example of those teachers in front of so many people? That morning, he'd taken his dad's gun after he'd left for work, stuck a partial box of ammo in his jacket pocket, and gone to fulfill his mission.

A stick snapped under his foot, bringing Mickey back to reality. He paused. Motionless, all his senses tuned into his surroundings. He saw no one at all on the playground or behind the academy. *This is too easy,* he thought.

Sylvia's class was located in the back of the academy on the left-hand side. That was why Mickey had chosen the wooded path behind the academy. He lay down on the soft needles under a large pine tree, peering through the scope of the rifle. He saw Ms. Willis walking between the rows of seated students. He lowered his rifle, placed headphones on his ears, and selected a song to put him in the mood. He cranked up the volume.

Mickey positioned the rifle once again against his right shoulder. When he was younger, before times were so rough, his dad had taken him to the rifle range and taught him how to shoot. He remembered his dad saying, "Keep an eye on the target." He had hated spending time at the range. But the training was finally paying off.

Sylvia turned, and he saw the baby bump outlined in her white dress.

For a moment, he took his eye off the scope. The baby was growing. Could he take the child's life? The thought briefly broke his concentration. *Keep an eye on target*, he thought.

Mickey's mother had left him right after he was born, and Sylvia would never be with him. *I'm doing the baby a favor.*

He was calm and methodical. He scanned the room once more through the scope. *There she is.* She was writing on the board. He placed her in the crosshairs and waited for her to turn so he could see her face.

She turned to face a student who was apparently talking to her. Her head was moving this way and that. She moved toward the window. He noticed that her shoulders to her midsection would provide him a better target. He placed his finger on the trigger and began to apply pressure slowly. In a flash, the shot rang out. The window shattered, and to his surprise Sylvia slumped to the floor. He had done what he'd come to do—get revenge. All it had taken was the pull of a trigger. It had been that simple. "That's what I'm talking about!" Mickey yelled over the loud music. Even from a distance, he noticed that students had started to panic and run.

Manhunt

Waiting for the rest of the children to file out of Mrs. Howard's room to do a search, the police officers waited in the hall.

Then Officer Bates heard the gunshot and yelled, "Everyone get out of the hallway and into a classroom." He turned to one of the officers crouched next to him and asked, "That was from the outside, wasn't it?"

"Sure sounded like it to me," the officer responded.

Officer Bates grasped the radio attached to his shoulder strap and depressed the button. "Bates to Central."

"Go ahead."

"246 at Mount Reese Academy. Requesting back up."

"Copy."

Officer Bates went to Mr. Pence's door across the hall, turned the knob, and swung it open. He maneuvered to the corner of the room where he could peer out with the least amount of exposure.

Speaking to Officer Martin behind him, he said, "It sounded like the shot came from the tree line over by the playground, but I don't see anyone there."

Officer London was still in the hallway holding back Justice.

Officer Bates yelled to him, "London, go down the hall to the other room and see if you can spot anyone."

◆ ◆ ◆

Officer London made his way down the hall and tied the dog to a pipe. He ran further down the hall and opened the classroom door. Most of the kids ran out of the room screaming and crying. One student stayed under a desk, breathing very heavily. Ms. Willis was lying in a pool of blood close to the shattered window. Officer London quickly crawled over to her and checked her pulse. She was shot, and bleeding profusely.

But she was alive.

Picking up his radio, he said, "Officer London to Central."

"Go ahead,"

"We have a wounded, pregnant woman. Send EMT," he said, trying to remain calm.

"Copy." The radio cut out, and then the officer at central said, "On the way. Estimated time of arrival is five minutes."

"She doesn't have five minutes," he said.

A moment passed before a response was heard, "An ambulance is en route."

Officer London looked over and saw the boy. "What's your name, son?"

"Rashad, sir."

"I need you to do something," Officer London said. "Can you stay here with her?"

"I'm scared," Rashad said.

"I have to stop whoever is shooting out there," Officer London said. He continued when Rashad said nothing, "I need you. She needs you. Will you help her?" He looked around.

Rashad nodded.

A coat was hanging by a hook. "Grab that coat for me."

Rashad grabbed the coat.

"Ok, what you are going to do is hold this coat over her wound." The wound was above the heart toward the center of her chest.

"I can't do that. I am not supposed to touch a woman there; I'll get in trouble," Rashad said.

"Trust me. If anyone says anything, tell them to see Officer London. Understand?" He said.

Rashad took the jacket and held it over the bullet wound.

"Press down, Rashad. She doesn't need to lose any more blood."

"Yes sir," Rashad said.

"Stay with her until I can come back with some help."

For a brief moment, Ms. Willis opened her eyes. She said weakly, "Thank you Rashad," and then she could no longer keep them open.

Officer London moved away. "She is counting on you."

With Ms. Willis being tended to, Officer London made it to the back corner of the room and rose up behind an American flag. He scanned the tree line with sharp, trained eyes.

His voice came across radio. "I see one shooter lying down under a big pine near the center of the tree line. And Bates, we have a teacher down in here, and she's pregnant."

"Is she alive?" Bates asked.

"Yeah, but barely. If we don't get a paramedic crew in here ASAP, she won't be." His words had barely finished broadcasting when another shot rang out, sending glass shards across Ms. Willis's room.

The shallow breaths from Ms. Willis erupted into three gasps of air. Officer London knew that she was dead.

Rashad's asthma got the better of him. He started wheezing uncontrollably and stood up. Another bullet shot through the window.

"Get down," Officer London yelled.

Squatting, Rashad took his inhaler and breathed deeply.

Officer Bates made another call. "All units, be advised. Perpetrator is behind the academy and is firing. We have him in visual." He immediately made another transmission. "London, take Justice and go out of the school from the left side. Martin, you go around from the right. I'll keep an eye on the shooter until you get into position."

"Son, stay here. Stay under the desk. Do you understand?" Officer London said.

The boy slowly nodded.

◆ ◆ ◆

Officers London and Martin's instincts kicked in, and they moved towards the sounds of danger. Officer London, with Justice, ran down the hallway to an exit on the left side of the academy while Martin made the opposite maneuver. They exited, careful not to draw attention to themselves, and made their ways around in wide arcs, attempting to attack the perpetrator from both sides. Officer Bates peered over a metal filing cabinet that he had pushed away from the wall. Two more shots in rapid succession sent him to the floor. This time, the bullets didn't enter the room he was in. He heard glass shatter down the hall; it was the windows of another class-room. *Damn, he's shooting' the place up,* he thought. *At least he's staying put. We might have a chance to neutralize him quickly.* Then a sobering question crossed his mind. *Are there more shooters?*

He grasped his radio and called out, "London, Martin, there might be more than one shooter."

Just then, the voice of Ms. Lawrence came over the public address system saying, "Teachers, Code Red! Code Red! Secure all rooms and lock all doors. This is not a drill. I repeat. This is not a drill!"

Get the Story

Mei Yun was growing increasingly fidgety. She had obeyed Officer Lemez's orders to take cover in the van after the first shot was fired.

Her cameraman, Steve, knew by the look in her eye that she was chomping at the bit. He grabbed her arm firmly to calm her down and asked, "You want this story, don't you?"

"Hell, Steve, you know I do," she quickly replied in a sharp tone. "This is what it's all about. The Superintendent and administration getting bust-ed for drugs is one thing, but nailing the scoop on a school shooting would push our careers over the edge."

"But Mei," Steve said, as if to provide some mystical revelation, "You're pregnant."

"God, why did I even tell you that?" Mei shrieked. "Look, we'll keep a low profile and just get some footage of me with the general area in the background. If we happen to get some action, all the better!"

Immediately, Mei's mind began to wander. She talked a big talk, but she was a mother-to-be, and her feminine instincts were stirring strongly.

She wanted to be a success. She wanted to be an inspiration to countless girls. One person, one woman, could make a difference in this world, and it could only start with her determination. That had been Mei's lifetime goal, but now she was pregnant with Sampson's child. She had to think of the baby and not just herself. However, she believed strongly in fate and that something or someone had brought her to this moment. If she made the big time, then both she and her baby would be set.

I'm at the right place at the right time, Mei thought. Whoever sent her that email was a Godsend. Then a troubling thought crossed her mind. I wonder if that email was from someone who knew what would occur—or worse, maybe it was from the shooter!

"Turn your head, Steve." She checked her gun that she'd concealed under her skirt.

"Why, hello, uh sorry," Steve said. "You never told me you carried a gun."

"There are a lot of things you don't know about me." She paused. "I am not your typical journalist." She laughed and said, "But don't take it personal; a mother can never be too protective, can she?"

"Who would have thought? A reporter who carries a gun," Steve said.

"And a Catholic. Mad world, huh?" Mei looked at Steve. "You with me on this?"

"I don't know," he shot back, grabbing the handle of his camera. "I don't feel good about you carrying a gun."

"Wait a minute, there is a guy out there shooting a gun, and you are worried about me carrying a concealed weapon?" She popped him alongside the head. "Would you rather me lock it up in the van and try to do our job without it?"

"I've never seen you with a gun before. Have you even been trained to use it?"

"Yep." She took the gun out, pulled the clip out, and slapped it back in. "I've practiced. After the baby is born, I plan on going to the range to practice on a weekly basis."

Steve put his hand on Mei's shoulder. "Does this have anything to do with Sampson's murder?"

She stopped and turned to look at him. "I promise you, I am going to find Sampson's murderer and kill him myself." *God, that's not very Catholic of me. Momma said the problems would not go away once I found religion,* she thought to herself.

Steve just looked aghast.

She turned away for a moment at the realization of what she had just said. "It's not fair that my child will have to grow up without a father."

With a determined focus, she said, "Don't worry; it is just another day in the field. I'll protect you if it comes down to it."

Steve said with hesitation, "Since you put it that way, but seriously don't become part of the story."

Mei Yun cracked open the back of the van and peered out, scanning the front of the academy for any signs of danger. She saw Officer Lemez enter the school to provide further protection for the children.

"All clear," Mei told Steve. "The shots came from around back. Let's go!"

Mei and Steve started around the left side of the building. They followed the walkway until they had almost reached the back, and then ducked behind a low-cut hedge. They didn't have a clue where any of the shooters were, but they wanted to maintain cover. Mei and Steve crawled along the hedgerow until they came to the end. They could now view the back of the school and playground area. They saw Officer Martin crouched behind a large tree.

"Okay, Steve. This is far enough. Let's get a shot of the officer and the tree line in the background."

Mei had learned several years ago as a rookie that she wasn't invincible. The lesson was etched into her lower left arm in the form of a scar from a shrapnel wound she had received while covering an active-shooter threat in Europe. She had been following a police officer too closely when the perpetrator had turned and fired several shots. One had hit a statue near Mei's arm. The bullet had shattered, sending a piece of sharp, hot lead into her flesh.

Steve was right on it. He raised the camera, pointed a finger at Mei and began filming. His shot concentrated on her until she gave the immediate details of the incident. As she began to expound on what might be occurring, he panned the scene. Just as he focused on the tree line in the distance, another shot fired. He saw the muzzle blast light up the shadows beneath the large pine tree.

The shot was aimed at Mei and Steve. But thankfully missed them both. Steve said, "Oh God! I see the shooter!"

Going Ballistic

Mickey had emptied his gun and needed to reload. He reached into his pocket and retrieved the ammo box. When he tipped it upside down, three bullets fell out. Mickey placed his last rounds in the clip. *This is kind of fun, and the Jags are gonna love me for it.* He aimed the gun and fired into Mr. Pence's room.

"Where is he?" Mickey said out loud. He should be in his room now with the students, waiting for the celebration to start. "Damn! I want that punk!"

He saw a reflection of the sun bouncing off a camera lens in the distance. "What the hell! Who are they?" *I'll shoot those punks anyway.* He stood up to get a better view.

Mickey fired a round at the cameraman. The round went through the hedge and exploded against the building.

A gunshot was fired at him. He dove into the pine-needle bed, but then he saw a police officer. "How in the hell did the po-po get here so fast?"

Then Mickey heard a loud command from his right. "Attack, Justice!"

He looked around and saw nothing. He turned.

"Aww fuck!" Mickey gasped. A moment later, a German Shepherd rushed straight towards him. Mickey's eyes were wide in disbelief. He rose up and started to panic. The dog was getting closer and was moving fast. Mickey gritted his teeth and closed his eyes. He squeezed the trigger.

He opened his eyes to see if he had hit his target. He had not, but he caught another movement coming from his left side. It was Officer Martin racing towards him. Mickey swung around and without so much as aiming he pulled the trigger again. *Click.* He was out of ammo, but it didn't matter.

Two shots rang out and burned through his chest.

Mickey fell back, still clutching the rifle. He could feel the warm blood running down his side. He made an effort to rise up, but was hit again with a blast of pain. Justice had arrived and latched onto Mickey's arm that was holding the rifle. Mickey felt the sharp pain in his arm from the dog's ravaging. Justice was whipping his head back and forth. However, the pain didn't last long. Darkness soon covered his mind.

♦ ♦ ♦

Officer London raced after Justice, arriving at about the same time as Officer Martin. London grabbed the dog's collar, gave a command and pulled him away.

Officer Martin made a call over his radio. "One perp is down. I repeat the shooter is down. We will conduct a search for other perpetrators."

"Roger that," Officer Bates called back. He radioed central, "Search underway."

When the area was closed and reinforcements had arrived, a dragnet of officers came from around both sides of the building and began scouring the premises. Only Mickey's corpse was found.

With the "All clear" announced to the reporters, they shouted, trying to get information on the tragedies, but then fell silent as they saw a medical team exiting the academy. The stretcher carried a fully-covered body. It was a pregnant woman. They loaded the victim into a waiting ambulance, which departed. Mickey was placed in a second ambulance and promptly left.

With order restored, officers and detectives identified evidence and questioned the eyewitnesses.

Officer Bates went to discuss the matter with Ms. Lawrence. "This has been a busy day." He paused before continuing, "And not a good day for you and the academy."

A public announcement was made about the Black Heritage Celebration. It would be postponed until further notice, by at least another three weeks. Grief counseling for both students and teachers were to be held for the remainder of the week. School would not resume for students until the following Tuesday. Teachers were expected to report for work Wednesday morning to attend crisis management training.

Dwaine would also have to postpone his plans. As far as getting revenge on the school, things had worked out far better than he had anticipated, or so he thought. The smile that came with the thought quickly turned to a grimace as Dwaine thought, *it is a shame that Ms. Willis and an innocent child had to die in the process.*

The Savage Voice spoke to him again. *But, do these people fear you, or even respect you?*

Dwaine could only think back, *no.*

Chapter Seven

Work Day

Teachers returned on Wednesday morning for a teacher's work day. Most of the staff was still emotionally reeling from the shooting, and many teachers mourned openly at the loss of their beloved colleague. Regardless, they were required to attend mandatory crisis management training. It would be an incredibly long and grueling day, and most of the teachers regretted having to attend. One teacher just sat at her desk, unable to focus.

Ms. Lawrence displayed a particularly sour face that revealed her sorrow and disdain for the past week's events. This was the second time in a matter of weeks that she had come close to facing her mortality. The shooting had amplified her emotional stress from her ruined wedding and near snake bite. Not only did she have to review the agenda for the day, but she also had to evaluate the police reports from the numerous incidents. She was not really concerned about the arrests of her colleagues, but she was very concerned about the fact that the teachers had not been adequately prepared for the crisis that had occurred. Further, teachers had not been able control the numerous students who had left their rooms during the shooting. Students had run through the hallways without any adult supervision.

Ms. Lawrence looked at her watch. The faculty meeting was in one hour. If there was anything positive about the day, it was that she now had a chance of being elevated to the principal's position, which she had been coveting for a very long time. She worried about how she would deal with incompetent teachers. *These teachers have a responsibility to this school. Can't they handle securing students during a crisis?*

At the faculty meeting, Ms. Lawrence had gotten a little of her self-confidence back. She lit into the faculty, "I have a police report here that says teachers allowed students to roam the halls during the intruder crisis. This is absolutely unacceptable. You put students at risk."

One distressed teacher spoke up. "Ms. Lawrence, when Ms. Willis was shot, her kids ran out of the class."

"Silence! I am speaking," Ms. Lawrence fiercely retorted, glaring briefly at the teacher. She continued, "You teachers are incompetent."

Mr. Pence chided her, "I think you are being extremely harsh. We followed protocol. My students and I remained hunkered down, even when shots were fired into my room."

"Mr. Pence, please wait until you are called upon. Several teachers did not follow the standard crisis operating procedure, and many of the students ran out of the academy under your watch," she raised her voice in anger.

"Students ran out of their classes when they heard the gunshots and other students yelling," Mr. Cleveland said. "It is pretty understandable that they would do that."

"That is no excuse!" Ms. Lawrence fired back. "Your job is to follow procedure. The problem is not the kids, but the teachers. The kids that left their rooms were placed in extreme danger. I will not have that kind of irresponsible behavior while I am running this academy!"

Rising on her feet to look taller, Ms. Lawrence shook from anger and frustration.

After reviewing the proper protocol, Ms. Lawrence announced, "Okay, we will role-play an intruder alert so you can witness proper student management during a crisis situation. Everyone go to the media center, and I will show you how to control a class during an emergency."

After two hours of intruder crisis role-play, Ms. Lawrence said, "If anyone here needs to see a grief counselor, please go to the counselor's office. Those who attend will be given extra time to submit your revised crisis intruder plans."

Later that afternoon, the faculty gathered to remember Ms. Willis. She had died of the gunshot wound at the school, and her baby had not been far enough along to be saved. The event produced a great deal of anxiety among the teachers, some of whom were questioning whether or not they wanted to remain at Mount Reese.

At the Police Station

"I have an idea," Investigator Candler said to Michael Gibbs, his boss.

Investigator Candler had spent twenty years on the force, and recently he'd felt frustrated. He had nailed several hundred criminals over the course of his career. But in the last year he'd been losing more cases, and his superiors were starting to take notice. Thinking through his idea, he asked his supervisor, "How soon do you think we can get a search warrant?"

"For whom?" asked Michael. "The girlfriend or the teacher?"

"Maybe both, but for now Dwaine Mann," he said. "My money is on that guy. He seems a bit odd. Have you read his record? He was involved in a shooting in the past. Granted, he was released on self-defense, but he is no stranger to violence. We are going to need to look at his GPS records, his home, and his phone."

Caught with Pants Down

The students were beginning to look forward to the rescheduled Black Heritage Celebration. On top of that, the dance was to follow right after the celebration program. The anticipation of those two events did a lot to brighten their spirits.

While everyone was excited about the upcoming events, the days leading up to them were anything but celebratory. The students returned on the following Tuesday to a heavy police presence at the academy. Metal detectors had been set up at the main entrance for the students. As the students filed in, Victoria was at the entrance overseeing their arrival and ensuring that the new search protocols were executed correctly.

The majority of students had arrived, so Victoria went into strict administrator mode.

"Fall in," she commanded. "Keep to the right of the hall line."

The hall line was painted on the floor parallel to the side of the hallway and was used to keep the students in order. They knew better than to cross it. Doing so would mean administrative detention or schoolyard clean-up.

Victoria paced up and down the hallway, keeping an authoritative eye on everyone. "Okay, everyone, head to your lockers and then go to class. You there! Too close to the line. Step over to the right and proceed."

Her love life and personal life had been crushed. All she had left now were the students and the academy. She was determined that absolutely nothing was going to disrupt this day. She was the authority of the academy. With Ms. Walker gone, she had to pick up the slack. Victoria knew that the county was watching her closely, and if she could handle this situation to their liking, then she might be named the new head principal. In her mind, ruling with an iron fist was the way to accomplish that goal.

She noted that Mr. Turner, the technology electives teacher, was standing back along the trophy case, waiting for something. Mr. Turner was a rather gaunt, older man with graying blond hair who was preparing for retirement in five years. When one of the students arrived and passed through the metal detector, Mr. Turner walked towards him and met him there.

Victoria stopped Mr. Turner and the student. The child looked miserable, holding his head down and pinching his brow together. She believed that Mr. Turner had taken that child under his wing to help him with an upcoming Young Technologist Club competition.

Victoria remembered; it was Jay, the student who had tried to get her attention a while back. "Smile," she said. "Last week is over. It won't happen again." The boy continued to look down and frown.

"Jay, you wanted to talk to me about something before," Ms. Lawrence said.

Jay looked up at Ms. Lawrence and then at Mr. Turner. His eyes widen for a moment, and he quickly shook his head no.

"Mr. Turner, what's going on?"

"We have club time this morning. Jay has a particularly tough competition coming up. With that, and the events of last week, he is just a bit stressed. We're going to work on everything, though."

"Oh, very well. Make sure he gets to homeroom on time," Ms. Lawrence said, dismissing the two.

"I *will* take good care of him." Turner smiled.

◆ ◆ ◆

Mr. Turner and Jay walked through the hallways until they reached his lab. Upon entering, Mr. Turner pushed the locking button on the door, but unbeknownst to him the button did not go all the way in and did not lock.

"I am so glad that you came today," Mr. Turner said to Jay.

Jay said nothing.

"You are so special to me," Mr. Turner said, while keeping a firm grip on the boy. "I know you will win at the conference. I will help you. You are going to be such a winner."

Jay did not speak.

After leading the boy across the room to an area behind several computers, Mr. Turner turned him around, bent him over a desk, and began taking advantage of him. Jay didn't move or make a sound. He was used to this abuse.

Mr. Turner had told him repeatedly and forcefully, "Don't tell anyone, or you will get in a lot of trouble. Do you understand?"

Just as Mr. Turner was finding his rhythm, a sound came from the door. Someone was there, knocking.

Probably a damn kid, Mr. Turner thought and kept on going, thinking the door was locked, "Oh Jay," he said to the child.

Preoccupied, Mr. Turner did not hear the announcement, "Mr. Turner, please report to duty."

There was a knock on the door again. Mr. Turner kept going, and the door opened. Dwaine said, "Turner, you are late for duty... again."

Mr. Turner rose up quickly from behind the partitions. "Yea, I'll be right there."

Dwaine started to turn around to leave when he saw another head rise up. "What the hell? Jay, is that you?"

A small figure stumbled from behind the computers. Jay quickly grabbed his pants and pulled them up. The child didn't say a word. There were only tears of shame. He ran past Dwaine out of the lab and into the hallway.

"Mr. Turner, you sick pervert! What in the fuck is wrong with you, man? He is a child!" Dwaine said as he closed the gap between the two men and brought his arm back.

"Nothing was happening; you know that," Turner said as he zipped up his pants and then wiped the sweat off his head with a handkerchief. "It's 'my word versus your word.' Hey, what the hell are you doing?" He stepped back, putting his hands up in an attempt to protect his face.

Dwaine brought his fist around to the side of Mr. Turner's face that his hands were not blocking. Dwaine's fist crushed his jaw. He continued the assault by blackening Mr. Turner's eyes and bloodying his nose. It went on until Mr. Turner fell back, crying, "You're killing me."

Dwaine's anger at Mr. Turner finally subsided at the sight of the cowering teacher, and he relented, then turned away to go to report the rape.

"It's my word versus your word," Mr. Turner called out.

"No, it's your word versus mine and Jay's, Mr. Turner." Dwaine left the room.

◆ ◆ ◆

Dwaine walked out of the lab and began searching for someone in administration. He had to report this abuse right away. He found Mr. Jenkins, the department chair, eating breakfast in the cafeteria.

Dwaine walked up to where Mr. Jenkins was sitting. "Mr. Jenkins, we have a situation."

"What is it this time? What happened to your hands?" Mr. Jenkins asked nonchalantly through a mouthful of food.

"I just found a sixth-grade student, Jay Madkins, alone with Mr. Turner in the computer lab. Mr. Turner was sexually assaulting him. I attacked him to stop the rape," Dwaine said, knowing that it was a partial lie.

Choking on his food, Mr. Jenkins said, "Follow me to my office." Then he paused. "Wait, where is the child? Is he hurt?"

"Heck if I know." Dwaine shrugged his shoulders. "He ran out of the room."

"Oh God. We will also need to inform Ms. Lawrence of the incident, so she can get everyone to look for him." Mr. Jenkins retrieved his radio. "Ms. Lawrence, we have a situation." No one answered, so he made the call again. "Go get cleaned up, bandage those hands, and look for the child."

♦ ♦ ♦

Mr. Jenkins found Victoria in the media center. She had turned her radio off while conducting research.

"I tried getting a hold of you," he said. "We have an incident that needs immediate attention."

"What's the matter now?"

It seemed that trouble never ceased to spring up. She had been looking for some tranquility, at least for a short period of time. It seemed that all hell had broken loose since her wedding and her emotional breakdown at the altar... all starting with the snake. Victoria took a deep breath just thinking about the chaos of the past several weeks. But she didn't have much time to dwell on her misery.

"Ms. Lawrence, we need to find Mr. Turner and Jay Madkins."

"Why? What's going on?"

"Apparently, Mr. Turner was caught taking advantage of Jay... sexually."

"He did what?" she asked. "Who reported this to you?"

"Mr. Mann did. He said that Mr. Turner was late for duty again, and he found Turner in the computer lab alone with Jay."

Victoria stopped working and called Mrs. Crabapple. "Mrs. Crabapple, please radio the police and get them in my office immediately."

"Hell, Mr. Turner is late for everything. He was late for the faculty meeting the other day." She stopped for a moment and cupped her mouth with her hand. "My God, is that the reason he's always late? I wonder how many students he has sexually abused. I need documentation from Mr. Mann stating what he knows."

Walking to the front office, she asked, "What about Jay? How is he?"

Mr. Jenkins said, "Mr. Mann said he ran out of the room when he walked in on them. We don't know where he is."

At the front office, Victoria told Mrs. Crabapple to make a call over the public address system for Jay. "Jay Madkins, please report to the office. Jay Madkins, please report to the office immediately."

When he did not appear, all of the support staff and teachers who had a planning period started looking for the child. They could not find him and a fear arose in all of them that he might be lost or hurt.

A student teacher found Jay peeking from behind some supplies in a closed off hall. The student teacher escorted him to Ms. Lawrence's office.

Victoria came around the desk and put an arm over Jay's shoulder for compassion and support. "It will be ok, just... I'm so sorry. All those times you were trying to get my attention..." she said in her most sympathetic-turned-regretful tone. "Look at me, child. It is not your fault. Do you understand?"

Jay only nodded.

"Your parents are on the way to pick you up."

Jay started crying. He feared his parents' reaction and shook his head no.

Victoria took Jay's hands in hers. "Your parents need to know, child. Plus, I'm required to tell them about such a serious incident."

Standing up and turning the phone around on the desk, Victoria pressed a button to speak to Mrs. Crabapple. "Where is Mr. Turner? And where is Officer Bates?"

Jay tensed up and shivered when he heard Mr. Turner's name. Victoria noticed his reaction and bent down, eye level with Jay. "He won't hurt you again, child."

"Officer Bates is on his way, most of the police were walking the halls and Turner has not reported to the office yet. Oh wait, he's coming in now," Mrs. Crabapple said. "Shall I send him in?"

Jay shivered again and glared at the door with terrified eyes.

"Not yet. I am almost finished with Jay. Have Mr. Turner wait in the east hallway."

Victoria spent a few more minutes comforting and reassuring Jay. Then she instructed Mrs. Beal, the school counselor, to exit with the boy through the side office door that led to a different hallway, out of sight of Mr. Turner. "Jay does not need to see him," she said firmly.

In calling the county office to report the incident, Victoria knew she had to report the crime as soon as possible. A legal investigator would be at the academy within the hour. Mr. Harrison, a retired Picks County judge who had become a special investigator for sexual crimes against children, would interview the teachers, the staff, and later the child.

Victoria called Mrs. Crabapple again, "Find a substitute for Mr. Turner."

◆ ◆ ◆

Dwaine had seen the boy escorted into the office while he filled out the forms providing the name of the teacher, student, classroom number, date, and time. He then gave a description of the incident he had witnessed. 'I found Mr. Turner alone in the computer lab bent over a sixth-grade student, Jay Madkins. I attacked Mr. Turner to get him off the student, who then ran out of the room.'

Dwaine ached for Jay. He had seen defiled children in the Middle East. Those children had had the same look Jay had. He could see it in the boy's eyes; his soul was wounded. No child should have to go through that pain.

Dealing with the Molester

"Damnit!" Victoria was upset that such a crime could take place on her watch. She vowed to make teacher vetting more of a priority. It took a few minutes for her to regain her composure. "Mrs. Crabapple, send Mr. Turner into the office now."

When Mr. Turner entered, Victoria pointed a finger to a chair facing her desk and said, "Sit down now, Mr. Turner. The police are on their way."

"Mr. Mann is a liar. He attacked me. I don't know what he said, but it's not true."

Victoria thought for the moment. *Mr. Mann is odd and eccentric; but could he lie about something like this? But what about Jay?* "I don't even want to hear it. Tell it to the judge," she countered with disgust. "You will probably lose your teaching certificate. Hell, you can pretty much kiss your freedom goodbye." There was a knock on the door. Officer Bates stepped into the office. He read over the statements from Mr. Mann. "Place your hands behind your back." Mr. Turner stood up.

"It doesn't matter, I will make bail. I will be coming back," he said. Before he placed his hands behind his back, he pointed his index finger out toward Victoria, with his thumb up, and moved it down like a handgun firing. Looking at her, he said, and then mouthed, "Bang." The only sound that was made was the metal cuffs clicking as they locked into place.

New Gang

Instead of laying low after the shooting at Mount Reese, the Jags were making a point to target people in the surrounding neighborhoods. Easy targets were their aim at first. Women walking alone had their purses snatched. As time went on, the gang was emboldened and turned to assault. They began specifically targeting academy students, since they put up less resistance. Violence had spilled over to the other races too.

A group of Hispanic high school students led by Luis Perez had figured it was time for action. They met at Mannie Hernandez's home because his parents happened to be gone that night. Since Hispanic teens had received the most harassment from the Jags lately, some decided to form their own gang, the Triads, to deal with them.

Parents had called the police on numerous occasions to complain, but very few crimes were pinned on the Jags. They police weren't taking the problem seriously.

"Listen up." Luis wanted to get this meeting started. Shouting over everybody, he finally got everyone to quiet down by making a loud whistle with his fingers. "We are being targeted by the Jags. Our people go to the store, and they get mugged. Our brothers and sisters go to school, and they get harassed. We are all sick of it." Luis was getting everyone riled up. "The police won't protect us. So we need to take matters into our own hands. We aren't gonna take it anymore."

"What are we gonna do?" Mannie said, looking at Luis.

"We go on the offensive. We fight back. We strike before our people are attacked."

Luis felt righteous. He felt ready. "We're gonna mess them up. Everyone here knows what this meeting is about. Anyone who doesn't agree, this is your time to go." Luis paused to give people time to leave… none did. "Can I count on you then?"

It started with just one kid. "Yeah."

"Hell yeah," said another.

All the rest followed suit.

He continued, "We need more people. You have brothers, cousins, and friends… whoever, bring them in. We will protect our people from the Jags, so we need to act fast before they get any stronger… We will take the fight to them!" he yelled, holding up his gun.

As the gang started to break up, Luis pulled his little sister, Isabella, aside and told her, "Go straight home. Get Lajuana and Maria to walk with you."

"But I have to go to the store first. Mama gave me a list of things she needs."

Luis gave her a stern glare that wrinkled his forehead. "You don't need to be walking alone at night. Jags like roaming at night; you know that. Walk with Lajuana and Maria." His voice was serious.

"Ok, I will," she said.

Luis and three of his friends spent the rest of the evening building up the gang by going to the pool halls and calling friends.

They didn't trust the cops, who were often callous, corrupt, and couldn't care less about minorities. People were beginning to feel the need to take things into their own hands. They had no choice if they wanted to survive.

County School Board Meeting

Dwaine was overwhelmed by the shouting. It was so loud that he couldn't even hear himself think. Many of the parents wanted the county administration to account for the recent problems. Becoming irate with the noise, president of the school board Caleb Cassick hit the gavel several times trying to get everyone's attention.

Parents were upset about the drugs found in Superintendent Nicholas's SUV. The county school-board members were very much in defense mode, trying to overcome the events that had occurred at Mount Reese.

Dwaine saw that a man stood brooding, probably thinking the same thing Dwaine was thinking. A dedicated teacher had been shot, and these people were bitching about drugs. Shaking his head, Dwaine could only wonder. The man went to the front of the room and tried to speak but was cut off.

Trying to distract from the situation, Heather Cox, a council member, said, "I would like to make a proclamation of appreciation to Officers Martin, London, and Bates for protecting our children." The motion sailed through without protest.

Mr. Moore stepped up and refused to be ignored. He was an upstanding business owner in the community and did a lot to help area students by mentoring them. "Wait a minute here. Those officers hunted down a child and shot him in cold blood, and you want to make them a hero?" he asked.

"Yes, we do. The student was firing on the academy. He shot an unarmed pregnant woman. What was her name? Ms. Willis, I believe?" It was Joseph Allen who pointed this out.

"The board will recognize Mr. Moore," Mr. Cassick said, rolling his eyes. "Sir, please follow protocol."

"I just do not understand what I am hearing." He paused, for a moment, and then continued, "I'm not sure the police acted properly. This poor boy was troubled, and they shot him. They just killed him." Mr. Moore genuinely seemed hurt for the loss of a child in the community.

"Mr. Moore," Shannon Greene spoke up. "We read the police reports, and clearly the boy made a move to fire at one of the responding officers. He didn't put down his weapon. He didn't try to surrender. He turned towards the officer with a rifle in his hands."

"We take care of our own. You should know that." Mr. Moore was getting frustrated with the lack of compassion for the child.

Mrs. Greene shook her head and continued, "The boy shot and killed a teacher and placed a large number of students in danger. That is a fact. The board believes that lethal force was justified in stopping the assailant, period."

"We are done with this issue." The president said.

Another demanding parent stood up. "What about the arrest of Nicholas and Walker? These school officials had drugs on them. They were supposed to be taking care of our children... What are you going to do to keep administrators from using drugs in the future?"

"Sir," Mrs. Anderson, the interim superintendent, chimed in. "That was an isolated incident. And these cases are still under investigation. Mr. Nicolas and Ms. Walker came up through the ranks and were considered exemplary citizens."

Mr. Moore was still standing. "Let me suggest that you start drug testing the teachers and the administrators on a regular basis."

Mrs. Anderson wasn't hearing it. Jose Garcia from District One called out, "I motion to table the subject until next month so we can formulate some type of plan."

Mr. Cassick knocked his gavel against the mini-podium. "The county will now open the floor for discussion on Ms. Lawrence's promotion to principal of Mount Reese Academy."

"I want to state how strict a disciplinarian Ms. Lawrence is to the children," said Jonie Timble. "I don't think she even reads the Individual Education Programs before she disciplines the special-needs children."

Dwaine had sent a fake email to all the board members earlier that day. The title of the email was 'Concerned Parent.' It had read, 'I am concerned that Ms. Lawrence is sipping whiskey during school hours.' Suzanne Johnson had found it about an hour ago, before the meeting. When she'd read it, a small commotion was created among the board members. As a result, Mrs. Johnson had approached Ms. Lawrence and asked point blank. Ms. Lawrence had denied it.

Dwaine went to the podium. It was a good time to embarrass Ms. Lawrence. It seemed ideal. He moved the mic to better capture his voice. "As a teacher, I have some things to share," he started to say, but was cut off.

Mr. Cassick gave Dwaine the floor. "The board will recognize Mr. Mann, a teacher at Mount Reese Academy."

Martin Allen didn't even want to hear it, though. "We all know that you two have an ongoing dispute. Your opinion is biased."

"You have no idea what I am going to say." Dwaine bit his lower lip, and his anger began to rise. "My observations and opinions are just as valid as anyone else's."

The Savage Voice spoke to him. *They don't respect you. You need to teach these people respect.*

Dwaine struggled against the Voice. *I am not hurting anyone, and that is final.*

You are weak! It answered back.

Mrs. Greene interrupted his thoughts, "Mr. Mann, are you with us? Mr. Mann, please continue. I am sure that the board would like to hear from a concerned teacher."

"Thank you. I have a problem with Ms. Lawrence being elevated. I have noticed that she is belligerent towards teachers."

"What do you mean?" Jose Garcia leaned forward.

"I mean she is hostile to teachers who are not in her inner circle. She is less than professional when talking to teachers in front of students. I know that you have received complaints from other teachers as well."

"Mr. Mann, you are the first teacher that I know of who has registered a complaint." Mr. Garcia looked to the other board members.

"Also, some parents have complained that she smells funny—like alcohol." Dwaine hadn't meant to say that. The Savage Voice came through. *That should teach her to mess with us.*

"This is outrageous!" Ms. Lawrence moved as fast as she could from the row of seats to the podium. Grabbing the mic at the podium, she said, "Mr. Mann is still upset that his last observation was less than perfect."

"Hey, I am just expressing some things that I have heard at the academy. I don't know, but it may be that sometimes she cannot handle stress very well, like on the day of her wedding." Dwaine followed the Savage Voice's lead but was not sure how far he should go. "She is unable to function appropriately under pressure."

Mr. Cassick said, "You do not have any proof. Moreover, neither I nor anyone else on the board has heard any complaints about Ms. Lawrence. Your personal spat with her is none of the board's business."

"I think we have heard enough. Let's proceed with the voting," Mr. Allen said.

Some of the board members were looking at their computers, obviously not sure what to make of the email. It did not matter. What did matter to them was focusing on evidence and not an anonymous parent's email and one disgruntled employee. But the seeds of doubt had been planted. Mr. Cassick said, "All in favor of Ms. Lawrence's promotion to principal of Mount Reese Academy say 'aye.'" Four council members raised their hands and said 'aye.' Five votes were needed out of the nine members present.

Heather Cox said, "I am troubled by some information that I've received about Ms. Lawrence. For example, Ms. Timble's allegation of her dismissive attitude towards Individual Education Programs… Then there is this email, and Mr. Mann's testimony."

Dwaine smiled wide. *Mrs. Cox is going to vote against promoting her.*

Heather Cox paused, thinking over her decision. "However, I have never had any issue with her myself. And prior to today, I have never heard of any complaints."

A knot formed in Dwaine's stomach. *Crap.*

Mr. Cassick patiently asked, "What say you, Mrs. Cox? Do we promote her or do we leave the academy without a head principal and search for a new principal?"

"What I do have are emails that contain praise from two other parents." Mrs. Cox studied Dwaine's and Ms. Lawrence's faces, searching for a hint to the right decision.

Mr. Cassick persisted, "Mrs. Cox, how do you vote?"

"I uh... I vote to promote her."

Dwaine went back and sat in his chair, devastated. *Shit! I fucked up, and she will have no mercy.*

Unforgivable Offense

Isabella left the grocery store carrying two plastic bags of items her mother had requested. She took off walking down the street alone. She had lied to her brother about going with her friends.

"He's not the boss of me," she said to herself. She was mad at her so-called friends too, for calling her a slut. *Besides, I can take care of myself.* Even at age fifteen, Isabella knew it was dangerous to walk alone in the hood at night; her brother's friend had been jumped recently. But she had done it before and nothing bad had happened.

Isabella decided to cut through the playground at Mount Reese. The wooded trail behind the playground would lead her straight to her neighborhood. Just as she entered the shadows of the tree line, she heard a rustling in a nearby stand of low growing saplings. A chill ran up her spine, and she stopped to listen, but she only heard the sound of the soft breeze blowing through the treetops.

She started down the trail and was just passing a large tree when a sharp blow to her face sent her plummeting backwards, spilling the eggs and chicken from her bag across the ground. The blow dazed her, and as she began to regain her senses, she looked up and gasped. Four boys were standing around her. She recognized them by the black hoodies they wore with jaguars on their bandanas. They were Jags. Kneeling over, two of them hit Isabella several more times in the face and stomach. She got one good hit to one of the boy's testicles. He rolled backwards in pain. Then two of the others jumped on her. One held her legs while the other ripped her skirt. Another ripped open her blouse. The foursome proceeded to take turns with her. Isabella struggled, but each time she tried to get away she faced pain. Each move to strike back was met with another punch to the face, another blow to the stomach, or another kick to the ribs. In an attempt to claw at her assailants, she ripped a patch from one of their bandanas. When the Jags were finally finished, all four spit on her and left down the trail. One limped home.

Isabella was trembling. She was in pain. She curled up in a fetal position and lay there for over an hour, sobbing and moaning. She eventually mustered up enough strength to crawl out of the trees and into the light of the playground. She stopped a moment to touch her bruised eye and cheek, and then she fell back from the pain.

An older couple was taking the shortcut from the neighborhood to the store when they heard faint cries down the trail and saw a figure lying on the ground near the playground. They rushed over to find Isabella beaten and bloodied, her clothes shredded to rags.

"Oh God," the woman said.

Isabella could not verbalize anything. She was expressionless, wearing only a blank stare.

"Don't just stand there!" the woman screamed at her husband. "Call for help!"

◆ ◆ ◆

"Hello, is this Mrs. Perez? This is Officer Martin. A young girl, Isabella Perez, was found behind Mount Reese. There was a situation, and an ambulance is in the process of taking her to Saint Augustine Hospital."

"God, that's my daughter! What happened?" Mrs. Perez asked in a frantic tone.

"Ma'am, an ambulance is taking her to Saint Augustine Hospital. Please come now."

◆ ◆ ◆

"Oh God. No!" She was hit with the realization that something serious must have happened to Isabella. Her eyes welled up with tears. She felt hollow; she had not been there for her daughter.

Sobbing, she dropped the phone and rushed out the door. She hurried to the hospital, ran to the front desk, and demanded to know where she could find Isabella.

The nurse asked, "How may I help you?"

"I'm Omiella Perez, Isabella Perez's mother. Please! I need to see her now! Where is she?" Tears were cascading down her cheeks.

After receiving directions, she made her way to Isabella's room. She gasped at the sight of her child's battered face. She rushed to Isa's side and held her daughter tightly. Isabella was still in shock; she didn't move.

"I am so sorry, baby. I should not have sent you out."

◆ ◆ ◆

Detective Duncan walked into the hospital hallway and saw Officer Martin was holding a plastic bag. In it was a patch in the shape of a Jaguar. "Take a look at this," Officer Martin said and handed him the patch. "One of the paramedics had found it."

"Jags." Duncan knew the Jags were trouble. People were getting fed up with the gang.

Officer Martin then handed Detective Duncan a report containing the older couple's statements. "Duncan, you need to see this too," Officer Martin said.

Once Duncan had read the report, he looked up and said, "Let's go talk to the victim."

They entered the room. "I am Detective Duncan, and this is Officer Martin. I understand that you are the girl's mother. What is your..." Detective Duncan was cut off.

Mrs. Perez cut him off. "Don't you talk to me. You people won't do anything, and you damn well know it."

Detective Duncan trying to placate her asked, "Just calm down. We would like to ask the girl some questions? We will find out exactly what happened, and we will arrest whoever raped her."

Mrs. Perez could not speak. Then she said, "Raped? No one told me that she was raped... But I will tell you what happened, Detective, is that she was beaten and raped by a bunch of thugs. You cops just go about your business while people like my daughter are left to suffer."

"Ma'am, we just want to find the culprits. We think that it could be gang related. We will only be a few minutes, and then we will be out." Detective Duncan said.

Isabella didn't look at them; she didn't say a word.

Mrs. Perez asked, "Jags?"

"We think so," Detective Duncan held the patch.

She said, "My daughter has just been through a horrific event. Your questions will have to wait until she has time to recover."

"But Ma'am," Detective Duncan said.

"I said not now!" Mama's face reddened.

When Detective Duncan turned to face Officer Martin, he shook his head and said, "Let's give them some space. We'll talk to the victim later."

Turning back to face Isabella's mother, the officer reached into his vest pocket, pulled out a card and handed it to Mrs. Perez. "If you can give us any more information, call me. The sooner we talk to her the sooner we can catch whoever did this."

Looking for Blood

Luis heard his father answer the phone. Usually Isabella and Mama were home at this time. He had a bad feeling something was wrong.

José Perez answered the phone. "Omiella, where are you? What? Oh my God! I will make those Jags sorry they were ever born!" Papa said, getting louder.

Luis had walked into the room during the conversation. His father was red in the face.

"Papa, what's wrong?"

"I am going to the police station. Isabella was raped by some Jags. I am going to see if I can get some answers from the cops. If not, I swear I am going to find those Jags and kill them myself."

"Those pieces of shit! It's time we stop taking this from them," Luis said. He stomped out of the room. He didn't know what to do. His baby sister had just been raped by the rival gang.

Luis walked directly to his friend Manuel's house, and the two began rounding up the other Triads. Had they acted earlier in forming a gang and fighting back, his sister might not have been defiled. His father was the protector of the family, but with Papa working all the time, the responsibility, Luis felt, fell to him. His sister... she was the neighborhood darling. The Jags had to be stopped. Hell, most of his people already wanted that, but Luis wanted more now. Much more... he wanted revenge.

Luis could not focus on anything else. Rage consumed him, and the more he thought about his little sister being brutalized, the angrier he became. Mannie tried to quiet him down, but Luis wouldn't have it. He pulled a gun out of his jacket and held it. "I'm gonna fuck them up!" he yelled. His mind began to race.

Mannie said, "You know I am with you, but maybe we should let the police deal with this. If we attack them directly, they will focus their attention on us."

"Police? Hell, Mannie, you know damn well the police won't do anything. Isa won't get the justice she deserves. You know that. We need to shoot whoever did this. Right now!"

"Calm down," Mannie said. "We need a plan or everything will go bad fast. We have the people, we have the guns, and we have time. Those damn Jags ain't goin' anywhere, Luis. If we plan this out, we can make 'em hurt real bad. Think about it, esé."

No one was safe. The Jags were making sure of that. Luis was going to gather the Triads. There was retribution to be dealt to those thugs. They would be sorry.

Still fuming, he said, "You are right, Mannie. We'll plan things out and hit those Jags hard."

Long Time No See

On Friday evening, Investigator Candler had gone through his old bag of tricks. He didn't yet have search warrant for Dwaine's home, and his request for a warrant for Dwaine's GPS record in the car was taking some time. Presently, Bill sat in his car and waited for any calls to be made. He wanted to gather more evidence before requesting a search warrant for Dwaine's home.

His receiver started making some noise. Bill perked up, ready to take notes.

♦ ♦ ♦

At his house, Dwaine pulled out his phone and dialed.

"Hello?" said Mei.

"Hi, Mei. This is Dwaine—Dwaine Mann. How are you?"

"Dwaine... Oh, Dwainey!" Mei said with glee. "Great to hear from you!"

Dwaine cringed when Mei called him that. He despised the nickname. He swallowed down his displeasure, but only because it was Mei. If anyone else called him that, it would not be tolerated.

"Hey, I wanted to tell you that your report on the Mount Reese shooting was great."

"Yeah, someone anonymously tipped me off that something was about to go down. It really gave me the edge I needed over the other buzzards." Mei laughed at the comparison.

Mei's voice was as sweet as Dwaine had remembered. He smiled at her chirpy manner and his heart swelled. Then he said, "Mei, I really need to see you. I think something else is about to go down at Mount Reese."

"Aw, you miss me, Dwainey?" Mei said playfully.

Dwaine nervously cleared his throat. "Well, yes. I'd love to see you. It's been awhile. But I also have some news for you. Like I said, I believe something big is about to go down."

"Wow, Dwaine. I'd sure like to know what you have. What do you need to tell me?"

"I'll tell you when I see you... How about Crane's Park? Say, around six?"

"Sounds good. I'll meet you at the fountain at six. Don't be late, Dwainey!" Mei giggled again and hung up.

♦ ♦ ♦

Dwaine took a shower and put on a pair of jeans, an olive-green shirt and a brown-and-dark-green sweater. He looked at his watch. It was only 4:45. He was ready to meet Mei, but he still had a lot of time.

He thought about Mei and how much he wanted to see her. That made him horribly nervous. There was a bar he frequented near the park. He could park his car there, have a couple drinks, and then walk the short distance to meet Mei. His nerves caused him to shake. *I could sure use a drink.*

At the bar, Dwaine's first beer went down rapidly. His mind raced. He thought about the shooting and how a young, pregnant teacher had been murdered. How did a troubled young boy get to that point? They had both needlessly lost their lives. Then his mind focused on Ms. Lawrence and her obsession with him and the Black Heritage Celebration.

By his third beer, Dwaine was reeling with a host of conflicting feelings. The White Guilt Voice was back, and with a vengeance. *It's your fault, you know. Racial tension exists because of what you and your family have done. You can't attend a Heritage celebration. That would make you a big hypocrite!* Maybe it was partially the beer talking, but Dwaine was having a hard time letting go of the past.

"Give me another," he told the bartender.

He swallowed down another beer and looked at his watch. "Son of a bitch!" He said it out loud. It was 6:13, and it would take him at least a couple minutes to get to the fountain. He slapped a fifty-dollar bill on the bar and told the bartender to keep the change. He stumbled out the door and made his way across the street. Ultimately, he had no choice but to head down the long walkway that led to the park. He was staggering and found it difficult to walk. As he approached the fountain, he saw Mei uncross her arms to look at her watch.

Dwaine cried out to her, "Mei!"

Neither Mei nor Dwaine noticed Investigator Candler snapping photographs of the two from afar.

Mei looked up to greet Dwaine, but her smile quickly morphed into a frown when she noticed he was staggering. Her suspicions were further verified when he walked close enough for her to smell the alcohol. "What the hell, Dwaine? Have you been drinking?"

"I had a couple," Dwaine said, under-exaggerating.

Mei was furious. "You call me to meet you and then keep me waiting, so you can have a couple drinks? I'm thinking it was more than a couple… Great way to kill a reunion, Dwaine."

Through slurred and stammering speech, Dwaine attempted to carry on a conversation. He tried telling Mei how he worked at Mount Reese Academy. How the place was a hell-hole. He figured that once she understood that, it would smooth things over. He was wrong.

"This was a bad idea, Dwaine. I have more important things to do. You can go back to your bar stool." With that, Mei flipped her hair, spun around, and walked off.

"Wait, Mei," he said while tripping over his shoes. Dwaine watched her shrink into the distance. He dropped his head and said to himself,

"You're such an ass, Dwaine." He looked to see if Mei would come back, but she didn't. He sighed loudly.

He turned around to go back to the bar. *Figures that I'd mess this up too.*

Back at the bar, beer wasn't doing the trick anymore. Dwaine decided to take it up a notch and ordered a shot of whiskey.

"Bad day, buddy?" the bartender asked.

"Bad life," Dwaine replied. He turned up the drink and ordered another. He wanted to cry, but he was too hardened.

The bartender sat the second shot of whiskey down in front of Dwaine and said over his head, "Can I get you something, Ma'am?"

Dwaine swiveled around in his barstool and saw Mei standing behind him, staring at him.

"No, thank you. I'll pass."

"Mei? You came back," Dwaine said.

"After I cooled down, I decided I didn't want to leave things like that. You said you had something to tell me, and I want to know what it is. Do you still want to talk?"

Dwaine turned his gaze slowly to meet Mei's. His head was spinning slightly. "Of course I do," he said.

"Come on. Let's get a table away from the bar," Mei suggested.

They chose a table in the back. It was still early, so the Friday-night crowd hadn't arrived yet. Dwaine began telling Mei that he suspected a gang war was about to break out. He was sure of it. "One of the girls, a former student, was raped the other night. And I overheard a student saying their brother is joining The Triads. Some Hispanic gang or something. People are just fed up." he told her. He also explained to Mei that he anticipated it would spread into other parts of the community, and it was bound to do some real damage to the kids involved, as well as to innocent bystanders. Dwaine looked away from her soul searching gaze. "Also there are some problems at Mount Reese. I... I wanted you to get the story first."

There was a long silence. Mei was processing the information. Then it dawned on her. "Oh, were you the one who sent me the email about the drug bust? Did you know about the shooter, too? Or is there something else?"

"No, no," he said before stopping himself. He looked at Mei with squinted eyes. *Crap, too much to drink*, he thought. "Look Mei, I had no idea that someone would be shooting up the place. That took me by surprise, just like it did everyone else. I did suspect the drug bust. That is why I emailed you."

"Why would you do that, Dwaine?" she asked.

"Damn it, woman!" he shot back. "Because I love you!"

Mei's face went blank and her eyes widened at the words. Dwaine looked at her like he never had before, with an expression that showed he was expecting the worst.

"That's one way to tell me." Mei looked around, avoiding eye contact with him. She had to buy some time to process this revelation.

Dwaine took full advantage of the silence. He motioned to the bartender. He needed another drink. In a short minute, newly-poured whiskey was sitting in front of him. He slammed back the shot and clanked the glass on the table.

A moment more and the liquid courage took effect. "Look Mei, this information was only an excuse to meet with you personally. What I told you is true, and the outcome will mostly likely involve a lot of violence, but there's something else I wanted to do."

"What?" Mei's emotions were churning inside of her.

Dwaine thought she wanted to lash out at him in anger... But on the other hand, she looked concerned.

"I wanted us to get back together. Mei, I have loved you since we first met. I just didn't want to mess up our friendship before—especially after the dorm incident. I wanted to get back together. I missed you."

Dwaine could tell Mei's emotions were buzzing. She looked flushed, confused, and angry all at the same time. She cupped her hands over her eyes and after a long pause she looked back at Dwaine. "Look,

I did love you too, at one time. I waited for you to do something, but you never did. Then you left the note and disappeared, and I found out you went into the military. Hell, at that point I figured things would never happen."

"And?" Dwaine waited.

"And today, I received a call from you to meet up, and I was elated. I thought maybe, just maybe, the spark would still be there." Mei paused a moment before continuing, "That spark is still there, Dwaine. I have feelings for you. It is just that things are complicated. Especially when you showed up half-baked, it killed it for me."

She continued, "If things were normal, I would. I don't know about a date...now." She paused and then said, "But there is something I need to tell you."

Mei stopped at that point. Dwaine hung his head low; he felt like a complete ass. All he had wanted was to be with Mei. But in this moment all he wanted to do was crawl under the table... after another drink.

"What is it?" he asked. He began to sink into depression until he felt her hand grasp the top of his.

Mei said, "Well, that's the thing. I'm pregnant."

Dwaine raised his head at the news. "Pregnant?" he asked. "By whom?"

A tear rolled down Mei's cheek. "Someone murdered my boyfriend. Actually, he was a teacher at Mount Reese too." The tears started to stream down her face. "His name was Sampson Damasks. I'm sure you knew him."

Dwaine's mood went from depressed to angry. Not anger towards Mei; just anger in general. *Sampson got what he deserved!* The Savage Voice hissed.

Dwaine worked to control the ire that was rising inside of him. It had pissed him off that Sampson was seeing Mei, but now to find out she was going to have his baby... *I need a drink.*

Wiping the tears from her face, Mei grasped Dwaine's hands with both of hers, leaned in closer and looked in his eyes. "Dwaine, you need to understand something. I will not have a relationship with a man who drinks. If you truly love me, you'll give it up." With that, Mei squeezed his hand, rose from her seat, and walked out of the bar. Dwaine sat there a moment trying to process it all.

He finally rose. He slowly walked to the bar and reclaimed his stool. "Mac, I need another drink."

"Coming up," the bartender said.

Dwaine caught the bartender's shirt sleeve, stopping his progress, "Not a shot, Mac. That's not gonna cut it. Just leave the whole bottle." He sat there wallowing in his misery and thinking about Mei's pregnancy. The Savage Voice spoke up. *It was a good thing you killed that Sampson scum. Too bad you didn't ice him before she became pregnant.*

"Shut up. I had no hand in that!" Dwaine said, a little too loudly.

"What's that?" the bartender asked from the other side of the bar, where he'd been taking an order from another customer.

"Nothing' Mac. Just hurry up with that bottle."

Message Sent

A message had to be sent. Too many people were trying to be brave and fighting back against the Jags. To address this, Carmichael put out the word that there would be a Jag meeting at the Garrison hangout at 8:00 P.M.

With their enemies increasing in numbers, they took precautions. The Jags almost always ran in groups, usually three or more. Not only was it safer, but it was also more intimidating.

Jags were easy to spot. They had been around awhile, and the black and blue colors of their hoodies were distinctive.

Four gang members set out to find dealers over by Waldrup Apartments. As they were walking down the street, Willy's phone rang.

Willy pulled it out and answered, "Hey man, yeah, we are almost to Waldrup Avenue. We'll find 'em. We'll make the drop. No worries.

Yeah, yeah, we will be at Garrison later." Willy stored the phone back in his pocket and the group continued towards the apartments.

Willy's phone rang again. He pulled it out and answered automatically, "Yeah, boss?"

"What are you doing calling me that, William?" An elderly female voice said.

Willy cupped the phone tightly with one hand and said, "Ya'll shut up! It's my grandma." He said it before they could laugh, and he knew they wanted to. Willy chatted for a moment and then stuffed the phone back in his pocket. "Guys, I have to stop by my grandma's house. She's wanting' to see me and she's only a few blocks from Garrison Street. Ya'll go on, and I'll catch up with ya there."

One of the other Jags spoke up. "Willy, man, you know we 'sposed to keep together, especially when we in colors."

"Ah man, shut the hell up! I'm gonna go see my Grandma and meet ya'll later."

Willy didn't wait for a response. He turned a corner to the right and headed down the dimly-lit sidewalk in the direction of his grandmother's house.

◆ ◆ ◆

The Triads were also out that night, looking for their rival gang's hangout. Luis told members not to engage any Jags they saw, but to simply gather information on where they were. He also instructed his members observe the Jags in order to learn their strengths, their weaknesses—everything about them.

Luis was with Mannie and two other Triads. They were patrolling an area of housing projects where they knew some Jags had family. The Triads, being a new gang, didn't have colors yet and dressed in normal street clothes. This was an advantage; they could blend in easily with civilians.

His group had stopped at a sidewalk near a corner of two streets. It was a major walkway to and from the projects. Mannie and the other two

Triads were busy talking, but Luis kept a watchful eye on the surroundings. To him, this was serious business. "Hey, ya'll keep it down," he said, not moving his gaze from the park. "We don't want to give our position away."

About fifteen minutes later, Luis saw someone walking down one of the walkways. As the figure drew nearer, it passed under a lamp post. Luis saw that it was one of them. "Boys, we have a lone Jag coming this way!" He did not speak above a whisper, but the excitement in his voice was evident.

"Luis, you said we were going to lay low and just watch 'em.'" Mannie sounded worried.

"Mannie, this is a great opportunity. If we take this dirt bag, we can get a lot of info that would take days to get." He paused for a moment, "Plus, he's alone! This is our chance!" Without moving his eyes from Willy, Luis motioned for two others to cross the street, get behind him, and follow him.

"Mannie, you stay with me." Luis's heart was racing as he gave out orders.

The boys crossed the street and walked down the opposite sidewalk until they were past the Jag, then crossed back over and walked behind him. They would intercept the scumbag when he got further down the sidewalk.

Luis and Mannie stayed in position. The target walked closer. At first, the kid just saw the guys behind him and kept walking at his usual pace. A moment later, Luis could tell that the Jag realized the boys were following him. The Jag looked over his shoulder a couple times and walked faster. He turned again to gauge their speed as he passed between two large oak trees. *Smack*! He was struck in the head by a metal pipe. Luis had knocked him to the ground.

They all stood over him, grinning broadly.

"We fucked him up," Luis said. He then gave the boy a solid kick to the ribs. "Get him up. We'll take him to the basement of my house and see what he has to share with us."

Two Triads lifted him to his feet. Luis gave him a punch to the gut, and he groaned in pain.

The group took Willy directly to Luis's basement and tied him to a chair. Luis paced back and forth in front of the captive. He was still groggy from the blow to his head. A large, red knot had formed.

"Well, look at the little punk," Luis said.

"Hey puta," Mannie said. "You belong to us now."

Luis turned to face his prisoner. "A real live Jag. You aren't so tough, you little bitch." He was enjoying toying with his catch.

"Come on, Luis, let's find out what this little punk knows," Mannie said.

Luis shifted his eyes to the Mannie. He wanted to savor this moment, and he didn't like being ordered around. He was the leader. But he also knew that the Mannie was right. They could get information about hideouts, schedules, and plans from this Jag. Even better, they could get even. They would just have to rough him up to do it.

Luis retrieved a baseball bat from a corner of the room and twirled it as he approached the young Jag. "Where is your hangout?" he asked.

The kid lifted his head, looked Luis in the eye, and spit at him. The shot fell short of the target.

"Hmmm, looks like the Jag wants to play," said Luis in a sarcastic tone of voice.

He walked over to the guy, moved to his side, at an incredible speed swung the bat with all his force. The strike hit the Jag's knee with a crack, and he screeched in agony. "Quiet, fool!" Luis said in a loud voice as he drove the fat end of the bat into the Jag's gut, causing him to cough.

"Now, you are gonna tell us what we wanna know. Or I swear to God, I will make this night one you will regret for the rest of your life," Luis sneered at the Jag. The thought of delivering more pain to the boy was really pumping him up. "Where do you guys meet?"

The Jag was silent for a long minute, then said, "Go to hell!"

Luis stood in front of him, patting the bat in his hand. "I don't want to kill you, punk..." He looked at one of his brothers standing at the

Jag's side and made a motion with his head. The silent directive was understood. He delivered a crunching blow to the side of the rival gang member's face. Part of a tooth fell out and dropped to the floor. The victim let out a loud scream.

"Listen, you don't really want to go out like this, do you? I'm going to ask you one more time." He paused. "Where do your people meet?" Luis lifted Willy's head with the end of the bat so he could see the boy's dazed eyes. He didn't answer, so Luis dropped the bat end, and then quickly drove it upward into the Jag's chin. "Bitch! Tell me what I want to know!" Luis screamed.

The kid's eyes rolled around in his head from one side to the other. He slurred, "Okay, okay. Don't hit me no more." As he spoke, blood gurgled from his mouth and down his chin. He tried to clean himself up by rubbing his chin on his shoulder, but that just smeared blood up his right cheek to his ear. He finally gave in. "We are meeting at a place on Garrison tonight."

"Where on Garrison?" Luis demanded loudly. He drove the bat into the Jag's chest for effect.

The Jag coughed and struggled to suck in air. "939... 939 Garrison Street," he said before dropping his head to his chest. He tried to take deep breaths through the blood and saliva that was pouring from his mouth.

"What the hell is going on down there?" a shrill voice yelled at the boys from the top of the basement stairs. It was Mrs. Perez.

"Nothing' Mama. We're just taking care of business," Luis said. The other Triads dropped their heads, hoping she wouldn't notice them.

Luis's mother descended the stairs and approached where the boys were standing. "Luis, what are you doing to that poor boy?"

"Mama, that 'poor boy' is a Jag. We're just setting' things straight, that's all. Besides, I thought you were at the hospital with Isa."

Mrs. Perez responded as she pushed aside the Triads that were trying, in vain, to block her view. "They released Isa. I just brought her home."

Mrs. Perez's eyes widened at the sight of the battered boy tied to the chair, and she began shaking her head. Just as she was about to demand his release, a loud gasp came from the bottom of the stairs followed by intense sobbing. It was Isabella.

"What are you doing here? Go back to your room. You don't need to see this," Mama said frantically. "Luis, your hermana has been through enough!" Isabella walked closer.

Luis suspected something more was bothering his sister than the sight of a little blood. He knew Isabella was tougher than to breakdown that easily. He walked to her and looked at his weeping sister. "Isa, do you recognize this boy?"

Isa didn't speak. She had placed her hands over her mouth and tears were streaming from her eyes. She didn't have to say a word. Her eyes revealed the horrible truth, and the affirmative nodding of her head confirmed it.

"Son of a bitch!" Luis yelled as he turned and marched back to the group. "You see, Mama? That 'poor boy' is one of the pieces of shit that raped your daughter!"

Now Mrs. Perez couldn't speak. Mama took a step towards the boy she had been about to defend and smacked his bloodied face. "You scum!" she yelled. Then she turned and went up the stairs with Isabella.

Luis was livid. "You really fucked up, man." He paced back and forth, still clutching the baseball bat. The others just stepped aside. They knew better than to get in Luis's way after such a gut-wrenching revelation. Luis tried fighting the tears that were welling up in his eyes, but a couple found freedom down his cheeks. "Fuck!" he screamed as he released a full swing of the bat into the rapist's chest. The blow knocked him and the chair backwards onto the floor. "Pick this punk up!" Luis demanded.

Mannie cut an awkward stare of disbelief at the other two Triads, and then they moved to set the Jag back upright. Mannie checked to see if the blow had killed him, but he was still alive... barely. Luis grabbed a plastic cup from the table, filled it with water and threw the liquid on his face. The beaten boy coughed and sputtered to catch his breath.

Luis squatted down in front of the boy and pushed his head up again with the bat. "Who else was with you when you raped my sister?"

He didn't answer. His eyes were rolling around in his head.

Mannie said, "Luis, I think he's beyond the point of talking."

"Let's load him into the car. We know where the Jags are gonna meet. We'll leave them a message, loud and clear," Luis said, still angry.

Two of the Triads untied the rapist. They carried him Tomas' car and dumped him in the trunk. Wanting more payback, Luis instructed the other three to get some guns. Tomas pulled out into the street, punched the gas and squealed the tires as they sped off. Once they arrived at Garrison Street, Tomas slowed down. They searched for number 939.

"There it is!" Mannie shouted from the passenger seat.

They drove right up to the front door of 939 Garrison Street. After loading the guns, they kicked in the door and rushed in. There were no Jag members. Taking a knife out, Diego ripped up couches and chairs. They turned the furniture over. Luis smashed all pictures and computers. Mannie found a stash of cash in the bedroom and took it. After trashing the house, they were ready to go.

Luis whistled for Tomas to pick them up. Tomas drove up and stopped the car. The three boys dragged the half-dead rapist to the yard and threw him down onto the dirty ground.

Message Received

The meeting had been moved back, and around 9:00, Carmichael and four others drove up. Carmichael personally checked to see if any cops were around or if anything seemed out of order. Then they noticed the body that was lying in front of the clubhouse. Willy just lay there lifeless. The five Jags exited the car and raced to the boy. They rolled him over.

"It's Willy!" said one of the boys.

"Oh shit!" he said. Carmichael ordered the others to get out of his way as he knelt down by Willy. He pulled the top half of his broken body up and laid him in his lap. He stared at the bloodstained, light-blue hoodie, and then looked at Willy's busted, swollen face. "Willy, what happened, man? Who did this to you?"

Willy's eyes were only opened a sliver. His breathing was shallow. He took a couple gasps of air in an effort to speak, but failed. Finally, he took as deep a breath as he could and said, "The girl we… Her brother and…" The words were forced through the foamy blood that filled his mouth. Willy never took a replenishing breath. He exhaled the rest of the air in his lungs and died in Carmichael's arms.

Confidential Information

A noise brought Dwaine out of his drunken stupor. It was Sunday morning, or at least he thought it was. He rolled over on the couch. He had passed out where he had been drinking the night before. The noise came again. This time his foggy brain registered the sound. It was a knock on the door.

He sat on the edge of the couch rubbing his eyes and trying to wake up. He felt like crap. Another knock came, this time harder and followed by a voice. "Dwaine, are you there?" It was Mei.

The sound of Mei's voice started Dwaine's heart pumping. He rose up quickly, knocking an empty whiskey bottle off the coffee table and onto the floor. He staggered over to the wall next to the door and braced himself against it, his head swaying from the booze.

Dwaine grasped the doorknob and opened the door. "Good morning," he said in a low voice. "Can't stay away from me, can you?" He ran his fingers through his disheveled hair without changing his expression.

"Dwaine, you been drinking again?" Mei shook her head and walked past the tottering figure and into the house. She scanned the room. Two whiskey bottles sat on the coffee table amidst a clutter of papers and an empty pizza box. A third bottle lay on the floor. A blanket hung precariously over the end of the couch. "Wow, I guess you have been."

Dwaine turned around to gaze on the disorganization. "I hope to hell you didn't come here to lecture me," he said. Dwaine walked over to the kitchen. He retrieved a used glass from the counter, filled it with water from the tap, and downed it.

"Always about you," Mei commented. "Look Dwaine, I came over because I have some news. I got a call early this morning that a Jag was killed Friday night. The gang war you suspected is starting."

"Doesn't surprise me. Those damned kids are always involved in trouble. What exactly happened? Some victim finally decided to fight back?"

"No, Dwaine, it wasn't random. At least I don't think so and neither do my sources... and apparently not the police either. I think it was an opposing gang member that killed him."

Dwaine filled his glass again and chugged down the water. He made his way to the couch, side-stepping a couple times in the process. Then he sat down and motioned for Mei to sit in an adjacent chair. "Okay, tell me why you think it was an opposing gang."

Mei took a seat after removing jeans from the spot Dwaine had invited her to sit in. She narrowed her brows, about to make a statement. "My source told me that the Jag had been severely beaten. But that's not all. He was reportedly left in the front yard of one of the Jags' hangouts. The investigators found blood at the reported site, but nothing else. Police don't think he was beaten there. The lack of evidence around the body makes them think he was dumped there on purpose."

"You think someone was trying to send them a message?" Dwaine pinched the bridge of his nose using his thumb and index finger. He shook his head.

"That's what it looks like. It appears this other gang used the victim as a warning. They wanted the Jags to know they were out there. They mean business."

Dwaine glanced over at the coffee table. He desperately wanted a drink, but all the bottles were empty. He gave his head a quick shake. "Well, I know the girl raped was a former student at Mount Reese. Isabella Perez."

Mei cut in, "Why would you think a rape would start a turf war?"

"The Jags have been harassing the Hispanics. The rape was probably the last straw. The boy that was dumped at the front of the Jag house was the initial casualty of the new gang war."

He continued, "Now, the Jags saw the outcome of the beating as a strike against them personally." He started to make some coffee. He looked back at her, "It is going to get a lot worse."

Mei had positioned herself on the edge of the chair with her hands on her knees and was staring at the floor. She checked out for a minute, in deep thought. Then she snapped back and said, "Wow, this could really be a big story, especially if these two gangs keep going after each other."

"Hey, while you're here, you want another story?"

Mei shot her head up to look at him. "Sure, the more the better!" She laughed.

"There is a man who works at the academy who raped one of the boys at Mount Reese," he said.

"A principal or teacher?" She seemed emotionless.

"A teacher. Apparently, he liked to bring kids in during extracurricular activities and has his way with them. I walked in on him while he was in the process."

Mei had taken out a small notebook and pen from her purse and was frantically scribbling notes.

"Am I going to get you in trouble? Who else knows about this?"

"Quite a few people know. I reported it to two different people. The counselor was called in, and the police were brought in as well," Dwaine said while giving the coffee table and the empty bottles another survey.

"Haven't you been told to keep it quiet?"

"Sure, probably, I think... but I don't care right now. What I do know is that, if you don't tell it, this story will never hit the media. There has been way too much negative press already with the shooting. I also know that if this doesn't go to media, that he will be charged, but the district attorney will probably cut a deal. Then, he probably won't stop." *Maybe you can fuck him up,* came the Savage Voice. Dwaine's face was grim.

"I'll talk to the producers. It will be on as soon as possible, after I have done some verifying. Dang, I could do a whole season on Mount Reese," Mei said, but her tone was not joking.

"I did you a favor, why don't you do me one? Stay here with me awhile," Dwaine suggested, already knowing what her answer would be.

"You know I won't." She smiled. They both stood up, and she hugged him.

Dwaine enjoyed holding her. Finally, he pulled away and said, "If I had my way, we'd spend every day together." He made a broad smile.

Mei gave a quick glance at the coffee table and the empty whiskey bottles and said, "Remember what I told you the other night? Get the drinking under control, and we'll talk." She paused and then continued, "I am saying this as a friend. You look like you can't control it. You have a problem." She and Dwaine walked to the door.

Mei turned to face Dwaine after he opened the door for her. "Sober up and get some help; I won't ask again," she said. "Bye, Dwaine."

"Bye, Mei." Dwaine watched her go. The skirt she had on made him hot. When she reached the front gate, the Savage voice thought, *She won't date me, huh? She's the one with the problem.*

♦ ♦ ♦

Dwaine was leaving school and found Investigator Candler waiting for him at his car.

Investigator Candler said, "You are under arrest for the murder of Sampson Damasks."

"What? What do you mean?" Dwaine said.

"Just place your hands behind you back."

Dwaine complied with the order.

At the station, Dwaine made his call for an attorney, Pamela McMichael, in the same room he had been in when Investigator Candler first questioned him.

Investigator Candler started, "We know Dwaine had a motive for Sampson's murder. He admitted that he wanted to date Mei Yun."

McMichael corrected him, "He said that he had dated her. Not that he was."

"We also have found evidence placing him in the Sampson's living room," Investigator Candler said. "We found a hair in the folds of Sampson's shirt sleeve."

"Here we go again," Dwaine said.

Pamela looked at Dwaine. She pulled out his bank statement and circled a debit card charge from a local salon and looked at him. "Did you get a haircut the night before?"

"Yeah, I was still itching the next morning," Dwaine said.

"Didn't you get pushed back against the wall when Sampson accosted you, Dwaine?" she asked.

"Yeah, hurt like hell," Dwaine said.

Investigator Candler was insistent. "You were with Mei Yun. We have pictures of you two. You had opportunity. You were there—the hair places you there. And you had means. Someone of your size and military training could have easily attacked Sampson."

Pamela chimed in, "It won't hold up in court." She smiled, "And you know it. First of all, you and Dwaine have already gone down that road before with the hair."

"Second, Dwaine weren't you talking to a journalist about some problems at Mount Reese?"

"Oh yeah, and there are some problems."

She continued, "We also know that the evidence and crime scene were tainted." Looking at her notes, she said, "Mei Yun had stepped in the still-wet blood. Even if Dwaine was there, there would be cause for reasonable doubt."

Investigator Candler grimaced. He looked at his colleague. "She's right."

Pamela said, "Until you have something solid, we are leaving." Both Pamela and Dwaine left the room.

Once they were out of sight, Investigator Candler bit his lip and said, "We really need to get inside his house and find some evidence."

Last Straw

Students were lined up at the door to the computer class. Dwaine gave them the go ahead. "Ok guys, go on in and start writing your assigned journal entries for the day. All of you need to read the standard. Break it down on your own, and we will review in a moment."

After the last child had entered the class, Dwaine noticed that Ms. Lawrence was coming his way. His heart skipped a beat. *Crap!* The mid-year observation was today. He quickly entered the room to quiet the kids down. He told them to be on their best behavior, which elicited several mischievous snickers.

Dwaine decided to get the class's attention. "Clap one time if you hear me." The students clapped once.

"Clap two times if you hear me." Two claps followed.

The class immediately quieted down. Dwaine turned around to find Ms. Lawrence standing in the doorway. "Getting the kids riled up this morning, Mr. Mann?" Her sarcasm did not go undetected.

Dwaine didn't respond. He just turned around and crossed his eyes at the class. He smiled suppressing a laugh. A host of snickers broke out.

"That's enough silliness!" Ms. Lawrence said in a strong and authori-tative voice. "You have work to do."

Dwaine began. "Someone please break down the standard."

"I will," Rachel said, and then proceeded to click on the small icon containing the document standards.

Dwaine walked over to one of the students to ensure the standard came up on his computer. The Savage Voice sneered in his mind, *She's going to make a fool of you again. You better settle the score.*

Rachel began, "The student will learn correct keyboard skills by using correct placement, the home-row, and proper technique."

"Will someone please tell us what that means?" Dwaine asked.

A girl close to Ms. Lawrence spoke up, "It means that we will sit up straight, put our index fingers on F and J, our middle fingers on D and K, our ring fingers on S and L, and our last fingers on the A and semicolon keys."

Dwaine asked, "And the thumbs?"

"On the space bar," she said.

"Great job."

Dwaine noticed that Ms. Lawrence had taken a seat at one of the computers at the front of the room facing the class. He bet she was looking to see if the standards were up.

She squinted to see that there was also an implementation plan for the standards. Dwaine saw that she noticed one boy in the back corner was suspiciously peeking over the partition. When he turned his head, she stood up and walked quietly to where he was sitting. Kids turned around and watched her as she made her way to the back of the room. The boy was playing a game on his phone.

"Son, do not use cell phones during school time," she chided.

Smack! Dwaine's palm hit his own forehead.

"Mr. Mann, your children are not on task," she said.

He went over to him. "Casey, can you pull up the typing program?" Dwaine asked.

"No." Casey folded his arms in defiance.

"I need you to help me out with this," Dwaine said softly while giving him a stern look.

"Nope."

"Alright then, come on over to the private seating area and do some book work," Dwaine said.

"No. Don't want to."

"Okay Casey, let's go have a talk." Dwaine looked up at the class and said, "Kids, start the typing program. We'll work on the group activity in a moment."

They stepped to the corner. "What's the problem, Casey?" Dwaine asked.

Before the boy could answer, Ms. Lawrence interrupted, "Mr. Mann, may I see you for a moment?"

"What is it now?" He spoke out loud, having meant to keep that thought to him.

"You have three more students playing around."

The Savage Voice began to stir. Dwaine had grown accustomed to the increased aggression and involuntarily clenched his hands for a moment.

His heart began to race, his head became foggy, and then he heard it: *Let her have it. Knock her out of her high heels. Right here. Right now.*

Dwaine spun around. "Look, do you administrators want teachers to handle the disciplinary problems in the classroom, or do you want me to send these problem kids to the office every time they act up?" He hadn't realized that he had raised his voice in front of the whole class.

Ms. Lawrence fired back, "You have to maintain strict class discipline. Every child must be on task." She continued to berate him. "I believe that, together with your last observation, you have exceeded the number of 'Needs Improvements' marks allowed. We have put you on a professional development plan. You have not made satisfactory progress. You are an incompetent teacher, Mr. Mann."

"You are denigrating me in front of the classroom. I think that might be an ethical violation. How about if we contact our ethics commission?" he said. The Savage Voice said in an excited voice, *Hit her now.*

"Take your best shot," she fired back.

Dwaine tried to walk away, but the Savage Voice struggled against him.

The Savage Voice balled Dwaine's fist again. But Dwaine took a different tactic.

"Oh I have not even started. I know that you have a problem with drinking. I know that Officer Bates has talked to you about it." Seeing the kids collectively turn around at the allegation was perfect. "I know that you cannot go thirty minutes without taking a sip. You are a drunk."

The kids' mouths just hung open while they looked up at the two arguing.

"I will not renew your contract for the next school year." The look on her face showed Dwaine that it was Ms. Lawrence's turn to briefly realize she had spoken words before the class that should have been said in private. Dwaine thought, she simply didn't care at the moment. He had ticked her off one too many times.

Dwaine didn't retort. He was too angry to speak. He just stood there staring at Ms. Lawrence, furious. He could feel himself turning red. Pain began surging through his shoulder and arm. Students just stared at the two adults with wide eyes.

The Savage Voice cried out in his head, *Hit her! Or I will do it for you.*

Dwaine's arm began to draw back as his fingers curled into a fist. He started to close the distance between him and Ms. Lawrence, but before he could take the second step, Rashad jumped out of a nearby seat and stepped in between the two. "Mr. Mann, stop, please. She's not worth it."

"You have some real issues, Mr. Mann, and you have no business being in a classroom." As soon as Ms. Lawrence spoke the words, she turned to leave the room. Before she walked out the door, she turned to face him again. "This is your last year, Mr. Mann. Your last year. And you will be present Saturday for the Black Heritage Celebration and to chaperone the dance."

Dwaine could tell that she knew he had a major problem with the event, and she was enjoying wielding her power over him. She wanted to get under his skin as much as possible for the remainder of the year.

Dwaine just stared at the now-empty doorway. He thought he was going to explode. He had to cool down. That oh-so-familiar White Guilt Voice crept back into his mind. *Just think. That's how your people have treated them for centuries.*

Dwaine tried to dismiss the thought.

The Savage Voice said in his mind, *If you aren't coming back, no one is.*

◆　◆　◆

Victoria went straight to her office. She pursued her lips together to form a tight smile. She had him. She took her flask out of the top desk drawer and pulled a long drink of whiskey from it, then sat down at her desk and accessed the teachers' report file on her computer. She found Dwaine's name and typed in the Note field, 'Contract not renewed.'

Tit for Tat

When the final school bell rang, Mrs. Howard left right away. She didn't have duty, so she was free to go. Her husband had talked her into a date at a gun range to practice shooting with a hand gun.

His sense of romance escapes me.

She was standing at her car door, digging through her purse for her keys, when she heard a voice from behind her. "Mrs. Howard, can we talk?" It was Carmichael.

"Sure, Carmichael," she said. "Hop in the other side." She unlocked her door and then hit the button to unlock the passenger door. They both got in.

Mrs. Howard may have been a new teacher, but she had an extremely soft heart for the kids, especially the troubled ones. That had led to some students taking advantage of her, but it had also earned her a certain amount of respect from others. She had heard the talk that Carmichael was a Jag. She'd even heard that he was their leader. But instead of feeling fearful and intimidated, she had reached out to him. She always provided him with words of encouragement and advice when needed.

Carmichael met Mrs. Howard through Willy, who had been a child of a neighbor. Carmichael saw right away how she helped Willy, so he had gone to her on numerous occasions to discuss personal issues. She had never ratted him out. He trusted her and looked up to her.

Carmichael was troubled again. Mrs. Howard could see that. He didn't offer to start the conversation; he just sat in the passenger seat fidgeting with his light blue hoodie.

"What's troubling you, Carmichael?" she finally asked.

"I guess you heard that Willy was killed last Friday night," he said.

"Yes, I heard that. Such a tragedy. I have been praying for him."

"You know how close we were, right? I mean, Willy was like a brother to me. Hell, he was a brother." Tears welled up in Carmichael's eyes and he turned to look out the passenger window to keep Mrs. Howard from seeing them.

"Yes, Carmichael, I know how much Willy meant to you. I'm sure justice will come to those who hurt him."

"Yeah, it will," Carmichael said in a low but determined tone. His voice rose, "Those bastards will get what's coming to them!"

Mrs. Howard was surprised by his words. She knew he was hurting, but that kind of attitude scared her.

"Calm down. It won't do any good if you end up taking things into your own hands. You might get hurt or even go to jail. You don't want that, do you?" She was desperately trying to get him to think rationally. "Besides, you don't know for sure who killed Willy."

Carmichael just became more agitated. He was hurting badly. Willy had been murdered and had died in Carmichael's arms.

"I heard who might have done this, Mrs. Howard. What I know is that it had to do with Willy raping some 'Isa' girl. I figure these goons are some of her family. They want a war and, by God, they're gonna get one." Carmichael couldn't hide his emotions any longer. He was weeping and using his hoodie sleeve to wipe his eyes.

"Wait a minute. He and the other boys in the gang were involved in the rape of that girl? You have to tell the boys who did that they have to turn themselves in." She thought, *Maybe I should turn these kids in? But, what duty do I have to these boys? And what duty do I have to that girl?*

She paused, trying to bridge the ethical divide, "Carmichael, do the right thing. You can't continue this war. It will ruin your life, along with everyone else's."

"I can, and I will!" Carmichael screamed the words. He flung the car door open and got out. Mrs. Howard exited from her side. She wanted to calm him down, but he was ranting and raving. "They're gonna regret making Willy suffer." He slammed his fist down hard on the hood of her car, leaving a dent.

Dwaine was just coming out of the side door of the academy to go home. He heard the commotion in the parking lot and ran over to see what was going on.

"Hey, Carmichael," he said when he noticed who it was. "What going on?"

"They killed Willy!" Carmichael was visibly upset.

Mrs. Howard answered, "He's upset. He'll be okay when he calms down."

"Don't bet on it," Dwaine said lowly, so Carmichael wouldn't hear him.

Carmichael, visibly upset, said, "I'm gonna kill those bastards!"

Dwaine saw that Carmichael was only getting more worked up. "You need to go home, Carmichael, or I'm going to call the police. You have some issues you need to work out."

Carmichael swung around, looked Dwaine straight in the eye, and said in a low and disturbing voice, "Go ahead, man. I'll get your punk ass, too." He turned and stomped out of the parking lot and across the street, disappearing through a stand of groomed hedges.

"That was intense," Dwaine said. "You should really be careful."

◆ ◆ ◆

Once Dwaine was home, he immediately grabbed a small glass and filled it to the rim with Whiskey. He sat down on the couch and took a gulp. He coughed a bit; that first drink always burned on the way down. But it went down smoothly after that.

Dwaine started thinking about Carmichael and the gang war, which made him think of Mei. The more he thought about her, the more he drank. Before too long, the bottle was empty, and he was passed out on the couch.

Sometime in the middle of the night, Dwaine was awakened by loud bangs, shouting, and other unidentifiable noises.

"Damn!" Dwaine struggled up off the couch. His eyes were horribly bloodshot from the whiskey. He staggered to the front window and saw numerous people surrounding his car. They were busting out the windows and the lights with tire irons. One figure was beating his car with a baseball bat, creating large dents with each stroke. Dwaine stumbled in the dark towards the door. On the way, he stubbed his toe on the foot of the couch, which sent him hopping and cussing across the room. He crashed into the door with a bang. He struggled to find the door knob, flung open the door and stepped out onto the porch.

"Hey! What are you punks doing?"

The figures stopped and jumped in a car parked on the side of the street. There was one person still standing at the front of his car. She lit a rag hanging from a Molotov cocktail and smashed the glass on the hood of the car. The bottle and its contents exploded on impact.

Dwaine heard a voice call from the getaway car, "Come on!"

"I'm coming," the figure said before darting to the waiting car, which sped off once she was inside.

It had sounded like Sharia Malcolm and Aleia Jefferson, along with their friends. But Dwaine didn't stop to think about things for long. He raced in the house and grabbed a fire extinguisher. Moving quickly, he sprayed the fire that was consuming his car, then surveyed the damage. He heard sirens approaching; one of the neighbors must have called the police.

A squad car pulled up and Officers Martin and Officer Lemez got out.

"What's going on?" Martin asked.

Dwaine said ticked off, "It was a bunch of punk kids causing trouble. They messed up my car."

"Did you get a look at who did it?" Officer Lemez was hopeful.

"No, I didn't get a good look at any of them. I just saw five or six jump in a car and race off when I confronted them."

Officer Martin placed his hand on the bill of his hat and repositioned it while saying, "It is quite a mess."

"Yeah well, my insurance should cover the loss. What are you doing working nights anyway? I thought you were a day cruiser."

"Ah, you know how it is. The city makes cuts to keep more money flowing to fat pockets, and we cops get to pull swing shifts." Both Martin and Lemez shrugged at the explanation.

"Oh ok, well night, Officers."

The two officers returned to their car and radioed the situation.

Dwaine turned at the door to watch them drive away. He had lied. He knew those voices all too well, and he knew exactly which little bitch had set his car on fire. He knew it was the Jags with her, and he suspected that Carmichael was one of them, or had at least been the one to order the vandalism. Jags had a way with paying back anyone who offended their gang or one of its members. And Dwaine had offended Carmichael big time earlier.

Sitting down on the couch, Dwaine reached over and turned on the lamp that sat on the side table. He was pleasantly surprised to see a glass of whiskey sitting on the coffee table. *Hell, I must have passed out before finishing that one.* He reclined back into the soft couch and held the glass of golden nectar up to admire its beauty, then gulped down its contents in three large swallows.

As he sat and basked in the warmth of the whiskey filling his empty stomach and rushing to his tired mind, the Savage Voice rose with it. *Those punks will regret what they have done.*

Chapter Eight

Celebration

The kids and teachers were working on preparations for the celebration. It had been rescheduled for this afternoon. A Saturday celebration would allow for more parents and community members to participate, which the school board thought was a good idea after such a horrendous events. It was damage control, and the school board felt the need to redeem the academy's quickly-failing reputation.

Sharia was busy ordering students around while they were hanging decorations in the gym. "Raise that banner up another six inches, Samuel," Sharia demanded.

Dwaine passed by the kids. He was still fuming over his car being trashed, and he knew that Sharia had been the one to cause a lot of his problems. The ride in the rental was more cramped than he cared to remember. Samuel acknowledged Dwaine, but Dwaine just gave a scoffing glare at him. He wasn't sure if Samuel had been one of the kids in the group last night. Probably not, but he wasn't in any mood to talk with him.

Dwaine looked around at the bustling activity that was wrapping up in the gym. As he stood there watching, he thought about Mei. He might have given the plan to scare everyone another thought if they were dating. But she would not commit to him. She had told him that she was pregnant with Sampson's child. He heard the now ever-present Savage Voice growl in his mind, *Sampson may have gotten my girl pregnant, but he sure isn't here to see his kid.*

You do know everyone is against you, even Mei, right? The Savage Voice then said, *Go to the trunk, we need to get something.*

Dwaine left the gym and went to his rental car in the parking lot. He opened the trunk and picked up a duffle bag. As he did so, he could hear the sounds of metal and iron. The bag was heavy. Opening it, he froze in horror.

Where did this come from, and why do I need it, Savage? We already have what we need to scare people.

Don't worry. I picked up some extra equipment for us. I have this under control.

Dwaine thought back, *I am not taking this into the academy.*

Dwaine's vision drew from grey to black, and he felt his consciousness slipping away. *What's going on?*

We are going to get the respect that we deserve, the Savage Voice answered.

Dwaine could no longer think, and he finally to succumbed to the Savage Voice's control. He was aware of what was happening but unable to do anything about it.

The Savage Voice took over Dwaine's body. *Time to party.*

◆ ◆ ◆

The Savage Voice fidgeted with Dwaine's ID card with one hand to unlock the teacher entrance. As he was heading to his classroom, Mr. Sellars passed him and commented, "What's in the bag, Mr. Mann?"

The Savage Voice stopped and looked down at the bag. He smiled and answered for Dwaine, "Ah, you know just some baseball equipment. I'm practicing with some kids at Statesboro Park in a while, and I just want to make sure I have everything that I need. I am going to just leave it in my classroom, that's all."

"Sounds good. Good luck with the kids Dwaine." Mr. Sellars proceeded down the hallway.

The Savage Voice watched him go. A sly grin crossed his face as he thought, *Won't he be surprised?*

Struggling to take control of his body from the Savage Voice, Dwaine agonized. There was an intense struggle playing out in his mind. On the one hand, he had come to embrace the Savage Voice that had been driving him to take action. There was no justice in the world, and Dwaine had thought a lot of people needed to be scared. It had given him fulfillment and purpose, two things he hadn't felt much of in his life. He wanted to surrender to that way of thinking – having a purpose. On the other hand, he was fearful of the Savage Voice's intent. His White Guilt Voice had begun to resurface and cause him a lot of grief. He knew even trying to scare people was wrong and the White Guilt Voice was chiding him about the pain he and his ancestors had caused others. How could he justify causing even more pain?

He shook his head several times in an attempt to stop the battle raging in his head. In his room, he unzipped the bag and pulled out a flask of whiskey. He removed the cap and took a long, deep drink, then leaned his head back and closed his eyes. He felt the effects of the drink envelop his wounded mind. Then he thought *I'm as bad as Ms. Lawrence.*

The Savage Voice, still in control, prompted Dwaine to take another long draw from the flask. Numb, he had made his decision. He was going to make Ms. Lawrence, Sharia, Samuel, Carmichael, and anyone else who had stood in his way regret ever crossing his path—regret hurting him.

Yes, it was almost time to get revenge. All he had to do now was wait.

Trouble in Paradise

The celebration would start at 3:00 and end at 4:00, followed by the dance starting at 4:30 and lasting until 6:00. Around 2 P.M., some students were bustling about rehearsing dances while others were in the choir room practicing the songs. Even down a separate hall, Dwaine could hear the kid's songs in his room.

Everyone was so happy while Dwaine was fighting against the Savage Voice. The struggle had been tough. He was barely able to get control of his mind and body by using an intense focus. It was a solid determination of will, but Dwaine knew any distraction could cause the Savage Voice to regain control. He feared the Savage Voice's plans.

Almost at a breaking point in the classroom, he unzipped the bag, pulled out a knife and was ready to slit his own throat.

I'll do it.

So, the Savage Voice thought back.

You won't get the satisfaction of the chaos.

What do you want?

Just control of my body. In exchange, I'll detonate the cars. You know I don't have a problem with causing a scare. But I don't want to hurt anyone.

It's a deal.

It was easier for Dwaine to be himself without worrying about the Savage Voice trying to take back control. But he wondered if he could truly trust the fiend.

With the bag in the classroom, Dwaine walked the halls observing various activities. He really needed to clear his head. Plus, he didn't like surprises. He wanted to make sure things were business as usual.

On the way there, he noticed a figure outside of the school in the corner of his eye. *Is that Mr. Turner outside? Can't be. Isn't there a restraining order against him? Is the pervert really that stupid? If he is here, I'll deal with him myself.* There had always been something about Turner that Dwaine didn't like, but after the incident with Jay, Dwaine's dislike had turned to pure hatred.

That's another punk that needs to be taught a lesson, the Savage Voice said to him.

Dwaine passed through a hallway. Worried that the Savage Voice would take over, Dwaine was engaged in deep thought. *How did this thing come to take me over in the first place?*

The playground should have been empty, but Dwaine noticed a group of teens in the back corner of the grounds gathered between the tree line and a storage shed. He stopped to inspect the situation. *Are those Jags?* Dwaine wondered. He squinted, trying to see who it was and what they were doing. One boy was doing most of the talking, and they would all occasionally turn to look towards the academy. If they were Jags, they weren't wearing their colors. Then Dwaine noticed something that the group of ten or so kids had in common. They were all Latinos, and all were wearing new red bandanas. "Damn," Dwaine said under his breath, "Those must be members of the new gang." Dwaine watched the group. Could it be that they were going to attack people at the celebration? Or attack their rivals? Dwaine would have to stop them if they came to crash his party.

Nervous, Dwaine had to think. Those brats were not going to screw up his plans. His mind began to analyze various scenarios that might occur, and he began pacing back and forth.

He quit pacing and walked a different way. Dwaine passed by one of the windows that faced the east side of the school grounds. Something else had caught his eye. It was another group of teens, and he instantly recognized them as Jags. There were about a dozen of them, some wearing light-blue hoodies and some wearing black. They were gathered in a bunch; it looked as if they were ready for a fight. Dwaine watched them. *Damn! Why have they have chosen the Black Heritage Celebration as the time to confront each other?*

Dwaine began pacing again and talking to himself. "Wait a minute. If those pricks are planning to attend the celebration, they will have to pass through the front metal detectors. That means they won't be able to bring in guns or knives." He thought a moment longer, continuing his analysis. "If they are going to knock heads at this event, they'll be confined to using improvised weapons or just fighting it out. Hmmm. Whatever they are planning, I need to beat them to the punch. Perhaps they'll even take the blame for most of my actions," Dwaine said to himself. The Savage Voice opined, *But Ms. Lawrence should know that it is you getting back at her.*

The Celebration Begins

It was 2:35, and people were beginning to arrive at the academy to attend the celebration. He decided to check one more thing out. Dwaine walked to the front of the academy.

As he walked, he noticed that the teachers and some of the performers entered through a side entrance from the chorus room into the gym. As he passed the choir room, he could hear the angelic voices of the students. He straightened up and smiled as he walked on. *If they only knew that one of his car bombs was perched directly over their heads.*

Walking towards the gym, he wanted to see about the security. He knew that Ms. Lawrence had requested that the Statesboro police officers be there, but there happened to be a couple of other big events in the city that day, and the force was short manned. The police captain had said he would send a squad car if one was free.

At the front entrance of the gym, lines of students, parents, and other relatives filed through the doors. Only two security guards had the front doors covered. The two security guards, who were off-duty police officers, did a good job of deterring most gang members. The word 'Police' was prominently displayed on the security guards' shirts. Having cold feet, many gang members simply walked away. But one security guard could be seen restraining a gang member for bringing a weapon to the academy. Only two Triads and three Jags made it in.

Dwaine went in and stood in the gym watching the people arrive. A voice came from behind him. "You made it. I am surprised." It was Ms. Lawrence.

Dwaine just gave a quick look over his shoulder and smirked as he turned around.

"I expect that you will be standing at the celebration today," she said walking with a smug look on her face.

"Yeah, I'll be standing at attention."

His thoughts of the events to come soothed his anguish. *Yeah. Go ahead and laugh it up, ya old bitch. I will make a mockery of you and the academy. Parents will be too afraid to send their kids to Mount Reese when this is all over and done.*

Ms. Lawrence walked up close to Dwaine and said, "You'd better be."

He could smell the whiskey on her breath. He backed away before she noticed the same about him. He wanted to strangle her right then and there. "Don't you worry, Ms. Lawrence. You won't be able to miss me if you try." He continued gazing past her at the incoming crowd, a slight grin curling one side of his mouth.

Ms. Lawrence puffed up as if she were being challenged. "Well, I have a lot to do. I'll see you at the celebration." She turned and walked down the hall towards the cafeteria.

Dwaine started to turn to go back to his classroom, but he saw a couple of reporters lining up at the metal detectors. They were carrying their equipment and needed to have everything checked manually by the guards. Dwaine looked over at them.

Once he was satisfied that none of the news reporters was Mei, Dwaine returned to his room. Dwaine thought, *Ms. Lawrence will be embarrassed on TV, good.*

We need to do something real quick, said the Savage Voice.

He opened up his laptop, pulled out the bottom drawer, opened a bag, retrieved the removable disk containing the jamming program and activated it. A transmitter was hooked up to send out the jamming signal. He pulled up the control panel on his computer, checked the status and location of the cars. The car in the gym needed to move right above the security. So, he moved the car forward another thirty feet. He then activated the remote-controlled car bombs and placed the remote in his pocket. Everything was set.

Dwaine thought, *I have second thoughts on that jamming program and the car bombs.*

Don't worry about it. It will just freak Ms. Lawrence out when she can't use the radio. There's not much to the car bomb.

Dwaine looked at his watch. It was 2:50, time for him to head to the gym for the opening ceremony. Savage Voice spoke again, *Take the bag with you.*

Why?

Don't worry; there are some fire crackers in it that we will set off.

He left his laptop on his desk and left for the gym, locking the door behind him.

He went to the chorus room entrance that was for teachers and students. There were a lot of students there, but no metal detectors. And no one questioned him about his bag.

The theme of the event called for an atmosphere of enclosed community, so the big, open doorways had been covered by two sections of black cloth. They were pulled aside for people to enter and would be released to cover the doorways once the event had started. Gold letters forming 'A Time to Celebrate' ran across the top. The rest of the veil wrapped around the gym except where the stands were. The White Guilt Voice tormented Dwaine ruthlessly, whispering in his mind, *Well, well... Dwaine Mannford, the hypocrite slave owner, at the Heritage celebration.*

Once inside the gym, he ducked underneath the bleachers. Leaving the bag there, he walked to Mr. Smith and Mrs. Howard. Mr. Smith looked at his watch and said, "Oh, it is 2:55. We need to get seated. It's about to start."

Mrs. Howard said, "Mr. Mann, this is my husband Jordan. He is a psychologist and owns his own practice. Why don't you sit with us during the celebration?"

"I am not sure that would be a good idea." Dwaine started to sweat. *You owe her some respect,* the White Guilt Voice chided.

"I suppose that would be best, on second thought," he added.

Dwaine normally liked to sit in the back at events to avoid attention, but this was a special occasion, and he wanted a good view of the entire scene.

Ms. Lawrence walked onto the stage. Then Ms. Lawrence made the announcement, "May I have your attention?" She waited. Then she continued, "Hello and welcome everyone. Thank you so much for coming out today." The gym became quiet. "Before we celebrate our heritage, let's take a moment to remember Ms. Willis who was taken from us. She had meant so much to academy."

After a moment of silence, she continued, "We are extremely proud to host the first Black History Celebration at Mount Reese Academy. It has been a long, hard journey, but we feel both privileged and honored. We wish to..."

Dwaine began to feel the horribly uncomfortable. White Guilt feelings were welling up inside him, churning in his gut and clouding his mind. *You should not be here, Mannford,* the White Guilt Voice said to him. He started to become nervous, and beads of sweat popped out on his forehead. Breathing became increasingly difficult. He loosened his tie. *That's enough! You told me to sit next to Mrs. Howard.*

Mrs. Howard turned to him and just smiled. "We have a good view of the celebration, don't we?"

"Uh, yes Ma'am," he said.

Up at the mic, Ms. Lawrence turned and introduced MJ. Looking sharp, he addressed the crowd. "Today we will showcase our history, our music, and our culture."

The students showcased historical events. Each era, along with its struggles and accomplishments, was presented with commentary from MJ. Then the Civil War era came up. Dwaine was silent, but he started to tap his feet incessantly. He was wide eyed, and his body started to shake. His ancestor was ever present in his mind. The White Guilt Voice mercilessly scolded him, *You racist coward. You are the great-great-grandson of a slave master.* Suddenly, he shouted to himself, "Enough!"

Fortunately, the background music volume was loud enough that most people could not hear him. But some did hear him. They looked at each other confused.

Dwaine buried his head in his arm. "I think I'm going to die." He whispered his thoughts out loud, without any concern about the people around him. *Snap out of it, Dwaine!* It was the Savage Voice. *You aren't gonna die if you do exactly as I say.*

Mr. Howard turned to his wife and said in an almost whisper, "What is his problem?"

"I don't know. He had some issues at rehearsal."

"He needs to come to my office," Mr. Howard said, quite concerned. He turned to Dwaine and said, "Come by my office on Monday; I would like to get to know you better. We can have a chat."

Dwaine looked up with nothing but a blank stare.

♦ ♦ ♦

Investigator Candler and a team of officers entered Dwaine's house with a warrant. Turning over couches and tables, the officers trashed the house looking for evidence. Neither the knife nor the boots were found. But Investigator Candler did find something that was very odd. In a locked office, there were pictures on a wall of a guy in military uniform with letters, written in an erratic and demented handwriting, spelling out 'payback.' The word 'Slut' was written on a picture of a beautiful woman. A picture of Samson Damasks had a drawing of a knife at his throat.

"Take a picture of that," Investigator Candler said.

On the desk, Investigator Candler and Blair saw pictures of a Sharia, Samuel, Ms. Lawrence, and Mei Yun. The word 'Next' was written on each one of them.

"Candler to central. We need to put an All Points Bulletin out for 'Dwaine Mann,'" Investigator Candler turned to Blair and said, "We need to move, let's go."

"Where are we going?" Eddie asked.

Picking up a brochure of the Heritage Celebration at the academy and seeing today's date circled, Investigator Candler said, "We are going to the academy —hopefully, to stop a massacre."

♦ ♦ ♦

MJ stood up, closing out the 1920's era. He then said, "And now the Great Depression, World War Two, and the Fifties." Students came out showing the icons of each period.

Dwaine popped a pill. After taking a moment to calm himself, he tried to relax. But even with the anxiety medication, he could not come to grips. "I really need to leave," he said to Mr. and Mrs. Howard.

He ran to the boy's bathroom. Despite the extra cleaning effort of the janitorial staff, the bathroom still smelled of rank urine, and nausea formed in his stomach. He could no longer contain the contents of his stomach. *I can't handle this.* His vision turned from gray to black, and then back to normal. He looked in the mirror. The image of Edwin Mannford from the daguerreotype appeared in the reflection. He turned his head left, and the image moved in the mirror. He turned to the right, and the image moved again. Dwaine looked into the mirror and tried to say in his normal voice, "I can't handle this..." but the voice from Edwin Mannford's mouth moved and sounded too much like the Savage Voice, a deep Southern pitch, verbalized into words "anymore."

The Savage Voice had manifested in the form of Edwin Mannford, and Edwin said, "I am taking control."

The celebration was wrapping up, and Ms. Lawrence came onto the stage. Edwin Mannford drove Dwaine's body into action. He left the restroom and peered through a crack in the veil. He could see Ms. Lawrence; she was addressing the crowd.

"Our time here has drawn to a close for the first annual Black Heritage Celebration at Mount Reese Academy. Please help me in celebrating our children's hard work and passion." The crowd of parents started to stand up and applaud. She continued, "We will take a moment to have all the students come back out."

It was apparent that all the work and time had paid off and resulted in a beautiful celebration.

Edwin Mannford silenced the nagging White Guilt Voice as Dwaine struggled to gain control of his body. But he could not. He looked to the ceiling, trying to clear his mind. His mind could not handle the stress of his White Guilt, or the constant dominance of the Savage Voice.

Dwaine's eyes met Carmichael's and the two stared at each other for a moment.

Another Jag sitting next to Carmichael grabbed his shoulder and pointed over to the crowd seated on the opposite side bleachers. Then Carmichael shot a bird at someone. *How fucking original*, he thought.

Dwaine looked and followed the extended finger across the room to two Latino teens. One kid made a fist and smashed it against the palm of his other hand. Dwaine thought, *This is my show. I'll just have to be sure to act first.*

Let's Dance

Edwin Mannford guided Dwaine, retrieving the bag from under the bleachers. There, he took out the flask and drained it. The voice directed him, *Scare nothing. We are taking revenge.*

The kids were coming out to take their bow. Dwaine knew he had little time.

He reached in the bag and took a closer look over his inventory: a knife, an assault rifle, a pistol, a shotgun, a bag, and ammo for all of the weapons. He reached into one end of the duffle bag and pulled out the bag that was underneath the guns. He opened it to find three chains and locks. He suddenly felt a great sense of power. He had everything he needed.

Then taking the bag, he slipped in behind the veil. Quickly, he pulled one of the chains from the bag and wrapped it around the inside gym door handles. He retrieved a lock and passed the shackle through two chain links, then snapped the lock. Everyone was standing and clapping for the students as they took a bow.

Dwaine had to secure the other door. He made it to the door located in the back of the gym, where he dealt with the second set of chains, locking them tight. He moved along the far gym wall, again using the bleachers as cover, until he arrived at the final door. It was located on the opposite side of the stage. He put on the last chain and lock.

Now he only had seconds to get back to his bag and set things in motion. Without giving it another thought, Dwaine moved out.

The two gangs had been ready to make their move, and now they started to attack each other.

Dwaine ducked behind the veil and withdrew the small remote control from his pants pocket. He pushed the button. The first bomb went off over the choir room, blowing a hole in the ceiling and scattering debris on the students. Shrill screams and panic ensued. The blast was even noticeable in the gym. The noise echoed throughout the entire academy.

Dwaine took the remote and pushed the button again. The second car exploded over the lunchroom, and the two front guards were alerted by the explosions. They tried to radio out, but the disk Dwaine had left his computer was causing too much static. Outside of the doors adjacent to the gym, a third explosion occurred overhead and knocked both guards to the floor incapacitating them.

Dwaine tossed the used remote to the floor, and he went to the duffle bag under the bleachers. He unzipped it and pulled out the assault rifle, slinging it onto his back. Then he took the pistol and tucked it into his waistband, behind his back. Last, he pulled out the shotgun and pumped it, loading a round into the chamber.

◆ ◆ ◆

The gym was echoing with frantic shouts. Ms. Lawrence had watched someone she thought was Mr. Mann cross the floor and enter behind the veil that covered the doorway. She had a gut feeling that he was behind all the mayhem. She marched across the floor and pulled the curtain back, ready to attack him. Instead, her eyes widened and several gasps came from her mouth in quick succession.

◆ ◆ ◆

Her arrival had surprised Dwaine, who raised the shotgun and released a blast. The slug missed its mark, hitting the wall above the stage in an explosion of brick fragments. She ran for cover. The shot sent people in the packed gym running in the opposite direction. However, when the first wave of people hit the doors to exit, they found the doors chained tight. The screams turned into panic. The kids, the parents, everyone was trapped.

Dwaine knew he had to move fast, before more police arrived. He stepped out from behind the veil and began scanning the chaotic crowd of bodies running back and forth in front of him.

◆ ◆ ◆

The two gangs had stopped fighting and looked for the cause of the gunfire. Carmichael looked at Luis, and then said, "We can settle our score later."

Luis and Mannie looked at each other and then looked back at Carmichael without saying a word.

Carmichael motioned for the two groups to attack Dwaine. Then Luis pulled out a wooden shank and stuck Carmichael in the back, twisting. "No esé we settle our score now." Mannie caught the other Jag unguarded with his back to him and stuck him in the side of the neck. The third Jag ran at them at full speed and without any type of coordination. Luis took the shank and drove it into the boy's stomach.

Falling, Carmichael pulled out a 3D printed gun. He only had one bullet, but he lined up Luis and pulled the trigger, catching him in the head. Carmichael looked at his loss of blood and fell back to the ground.

◆ ◆ ◆

A parent started marching with fierce determination straight towards Dwaine, pushing frantic people aside along the way. Dwaine swung the gun around and let loose a blast. The parent ducked to the ground, quickly stood up, and continued towards him. Coming at Dwaine with more speed, he hit Dwaine as hard as he could in the face. Dwaine shook off a bloody nose and raised the shotgun again. They struggled with the gun when Dwaine head butt him temporarily disorientating the parent. He raised the gun and fired a shot that hit the parent in the chest. The bullet exited through the man's back.

The screams intensified as Dwaine began moving forward into the center of the gym, where he could get a better view. It was difficult to find his targets in the ocean of panicked people. Then he noticed Sharia and Samuel moving in front of the bleachers towards the stage. He raised the shotgun and fired another two shells in rapid succession. The first shot hit a man crossing in front of Dwaine, blowing his shoulder off. The second slug found its mark, entering Samuel's side and ripping through him. Dwaine immediately marched towards his victim, pumping the shotgun as he went.

You were supposed to just scare people, admonished the White Guilt Voice.

Scare people my ass. This is about getting revenge on all those who have hurt me, Dwaine retorted. Samuel was lying in a pool of blood. Blood was seeping out of his side, and he was gasping for air. Then he stopped breathing. Sharia sat by his side with her head between her legs and arms over her head. She was weeping uncontrollably. Dwaine kicked her leg, and she looked up at him with a face that projected both fear and deep hatred.

Dwaine said, "It's a shame you killed Samuel."

Sharia added to her distorted face a look of bewilderment.

"That's right. You are the one that put him up to setting off the bomb in my room, which got my ass chewed out. Oh yeah, and you set my car on fire, bitch!"

"Fuck you, Mr. Mann!" Sharia screamed in a stream of tears.

"Fuck me?" He dropped the shotgun inches away from her face and pulled the trigger. *Click.* Sharia held her eyes closed tightly for a couple of seemingly endless seconds. The gun hadn't fired. Dwaine needed to reload. Instead, she opened her eyes to see him standing there with the pistol pointed at her forehead. "Die, you spoiled little bitch!" He fired. Skull fragments went on the floor and wall.

Dwaine spun around to the sound of people beating at the main doors. Someone was using a fire extinguisher to try and bash the heavy chain. He took several long strides towards the center of the gym, turned in the direction of the doors and fired three shots into the crowd. One bullet struck a girl in the side of the head, one dropped a boy that was directly behind her, and the third slug tore through the arm of the man with the extinguisher. His light-blue shirt covered with red.

"Now, where in the hell is Ms. Lawrence? She must be hiding." Dwaine turned his attention towards the stage. He wondered if she could be hiding behind the veil or the bleachers. Where ever she was, she couldn't be hard to miss; she was wearing a bright yellow blouse. People were darting back and forth in front of the stage, blocking his vision. Frustrated that he could not find her, he said, "That's it!" tucking the pistol back into the back of his pants. He grabbed the hand guard of the assault rifle and added a magazine, then swung it into position and released a spray of bullets into the crowd. More bodies tumbled across the gym. Blood splattered on the walls and spilled across the floor.

The rapid blasts had startled Ms. Lawrence, who was on the gym floor trying to hide behind the speakers on the stage. Dwaine grinned. His heart raced. *There she is.* It was time to make her pay.

Dwaine walked up the steps onto the stage and then over to the speakers. He tumbled the stacked speakers to the floor with a strong kick. Ms. Lawrence crouched there, looking up at him in fear and anger. He jumped off of the stage.

"You poor pathetic soul." She clenched her teeth and stood up, standing her ground. She then began to laugh. "You are a pathetic racist and a psychotic murderer!"

Dwaine took a step closer to her and pointed the rifle at her face. "Yeah, who is the pathetic one now?"

The White Guilt Voice was shouting in his head. *Edwin Mannford, you were here all along, weren't you?*

Yes.

Dwaine's body began to shake. The real Dwaine struggled to regain control, but could not.

"You are really messed up, Mr. Mann," Ms. Lawrence said, not caring at this point that an assault rifle was aimed at her. "Disconnected from reality and demented."

"Oh, just so you know, I put the snake in your office," Dwaine said.

She glared at him. Her eyes were on fire.

He continued, "I was the one who fucked up your wedding day."

In an act of defiance and sheer will to live, she ran towards him.

He took a firm grip on the assault rifle and pulled the trigger, wanting to spray her with hot lead. Instead, the gun jammed. "Shit!" he shrieked, flinging the rifle on to the stage.

She tripped into to the speaker. It gave him just enough time.

Dwaine took several steps back and pulled the pistol from behind his back, brought it around and pointed it at Ms. Lawrence, who stopped with the gun point-blank against her head.

Savoring this opportunity, Dwaine lowered the gun to her left leg, and she took that opportunity to attack. She grabbed his arm and bit tearing into his skin. Pain gripped Dwaine. He could not shake her. She tried to dislodge the gun in his hand, but she could not. The struggle was short lived. Balling his hand into a fist, he punched her in the face. She barely held on. He used the gun she was desperately trying to dislodge and fired once into her kneecap. She stumbled to the ground.

"How does it feel not to have any control? How does it feel to be at my mercy?"

Seeing her leg spurting blood, she could no longer maintain her defiance. She grabbed her knee with both of her hands. "Please... my family... Aaron," was all she could say. Her face was pleading. "Please."

"Your family? Your family means nothing," Dwaine spoke. "Aaron, the fiancé? You left him at the altar."

"We are..." she said.

Dwaine would not hear her pleading. Standing above her, his face was blank. He had no emotions. He fired two rapid rounds into her head. Her body fell backwards from the impact, limp.

Dwaine turned around slowly and stood there on the gym floor for a moment.

He watched the poor, whimpering mass of terrorized people screaming and crying. He had a crazed look in his eyes.

Where in the hell is Turner? He scanned the crowd. He didn't see Turner, but at that point it didn't really matter. He looked across the gym.

Dwaine's persona briefly surfaced as he saw a boy that had been shot. Jay lay on the ground with a bullet in his head.

♦ ♦ ♦

Mrs. Howard saw Mr. Mann attacking students and parents. She reached into her purse for her gun and aimed at Dwaine.

She could not understand why Dwaine was attacking. He looked different, as if he were a crazed man. Her hands trembled. Instead of firing, she thought for a moment about what it would mean to take Dwaine's life. And she froze.

A bullet flew her way and her husband jumped on her. Her gun fell to the floor. He took her hand, and they scurried away for a moment of respite from the insanity. They hid behind the stands, cowering.

More gunshots rang out. Mr. Howard said, "I can't let him get away with this."

"Where's your gun?" Mrs. Howard asked.

He shook his head and said, "It's being repaired." He looked at their attacker and the people being slaughtered then looked back at her and said, "I love you."

Knowing what he meant, she pleaded with him, "No, stay here. The police will be here soon." Looking for her gun, she finally found it under a table. Her clip was five feet from the gun.

Her husband ran out to tackle Dwaine while she went to get her gun and clip.

But before Mrs. Howard's husband could attack him, Dwaine sent a slug into his chest.

♦ ♦ ♦

He had it coming; he shouldn't have tried to be a hero, Dwaine thought.

"You sick bastard!" Some woman, he could not tell who, was now holding a gun. He sent a salvo of bullets her way, and she scurried away. She had a look of pain as she ran trying to escape her death.

Ready to finish the job on her and the rest of the people in the gym, he reloaded his weapon. The pistol in hand, he was now ready, and he took aim.

Suddenly, a voice called out from behind him, "Mr. Mann, stop!"

He swung around to see Rashad standing on the stage. The young, once-timid boy now towered over Dwaine from his elevated position. And he sounded strong and in control. Rashad was holding the assault rifle that Dwaine had tossed aside.

A small chuckle came from Dwaine as he considered the irony. "Who taught you to focus, Rashad?"

"You did."

"And who taught you to remain calm in tense situations?"

"You did... Mr. Mann, your voice. It sounds different. You need help."

"You should hide. I am taking revenge," Dwaine spoke.

Dwaine grinned, then looked to his left and then to his right. People were lying in agony all around him, moaning and weeping. He tightened his grip on the pistol, but before he could raise it, the White Guilt Voice filled his mind. *He is a child and your friend*. Dwaine hesitated.

"Don't do it, Mr. Mann. It's over. Put the gun down," Rashad said, holding the assault rifle on Dwaine. Rashad could tell that Mr. Mann was struggling with some major mental demons. His eyes were bloodshot. They darted from right to left, then back again. "Come on, Mr. Mann. Let's end this."

"You won't pull the trigger," Dwaine said in a harsh voice. In one sweeping motion, Dwaine raised the pistol at Rashad and pulled the trigger. At the same time, Rashad let two bursts go from the assault rifle in an automatic reaction.

But the pistol bullet missed.

Rashad's two rounds drove into Dwaine's chest, knocking him to the floor. Dwaine laid there, his life slowly leaving his body.

♦ ♦ ♦

Rashad could not believe what he had done. His friend was shot, and he had pulled the trigger. "You shouldn't have done it," Rashad said remorsefully as he stood over Dwaine's body.

The police, including Investigator Candler and Eddie Blair, had arrived and were trying to open the main door. Rashad saw that the door was not giving way to their forceful pounding. Then the police shot the glass out of the window pane on the door. Reaching through the hole, Investigator Candler aimed a gun at the chain and fired.

Rashad moved towards the door and was about to lay the rifle on the floor when he noticed a figure standing outside, just beyond one of the gym windows. The man raised his assault rifle and Rashad yelled, "Get down! Hide!" Rashad brought up the assault rifle to shoot.

◆ ◆ ◆

Mr. Turner had heard shots as he walked up to the gym. At the window, he scanned the area. *Damn, someone did a number here, but Mr. Mann and Ms. Lawrence better not have been shot. They are mine.* He looked, and then he saw them. Both of them were on the floor. Were they dead? His anger was boiling. He did not know if his revenge was taken away from him. With all the anger he could muster, he aimed at the survivors. "I will kill you all." He took aim at a child and fired.

◆ ◆ ◆

Before Rashad could take aim and pull the trigger, Mr. Turner sprayed numerous rounds through the glass, which shattered and sent fragments cascading through the gym.

Rashad was hit in the thigh, and the sudden blast sent him to the floor. He recovered and painfully rose up onto one knee, aiming at Mr. Turner. But before he could fire, a barrage of bullets hit Mr. Turner, dropping him to the ground.

Mrs. Howard had fired an entire clip of bullets in Mr. Turner's direction.

♦ ♦ ♦

Rushing in behind the police were Mei and Steve. They had heard over their radio that an All Points Bulletin was issued for Dwaine Mann at the school, and they had hastened to get to the academy. Mei yelled at Steve to start filming. She looked around at the scene. Bodies were lying about the gym. Huddled masses of survivors were weeping hysterically.

Then she noticed Dwaine lying in the center of the room. She cried out, "Dwaine!" and rushed to his side. Bending over his bloodied body, she knew he was dead. Mei Yun hung her head and wept.

Suddenly, she felt a stirring from Dwaine. He had moved just a little. Mei looked up.

"Dwaine, can you hear me?" she asked. Then she saw it—the malicious blankness etched on Dwaine's face. A hand shot up and grabbed her by the throat.

Then she heard, "You," a sneer was on his face. "I want you to know something... I killed Sampson. If I can't have you then no one can," Dwaine could barely whisper. But his grip was getting tighter.

Mei tried to move back. But she could not. "Plea..."

He would not let go.

His hand felt like a vice around her throat as she struggled to gasp for air. She was turning blue in the face. She tried to reach for her gun, but she could not grab it. She had a second or two before she would lose consciousness. Reaching for the gun again, she was able to pull it free from her holster. She took her gun and forced it against his head and pulled the trigger. She heard the blast. Smoke came from her barrel. She looked over to see a bullet wound to Dwaine's head. His arm dropped to the floor.

"For Sampson."

Connections

Mei dropped her gun. She stood up and covered her mouth. Her friend was gone, and he had tried to kill her. Pinching her lips together, she said her last words to Dwaine Mann. "I hope those demons let you go now."

She saw a young man looking at Dwaine's body. "He was my friend," he said, now looking up at her.

She helped him to stand. Then she asked, "How did you know him?"

"He helped me. He made me feel normal. He connected with me when no one else could or would," Rashad said, looking at Mei. "He helped me against the bullies, but in the end he became the bully. I don't get it."

Chapter Nine

Vigil

Makeshift memorials popped up all along the sidewalks for the students. One memorial was for a young girl, featuring peppermints and snap dragons because of her love of the candy and the flower.

The mourners came from around the state and from all parts of the nation. They all wondered how a teacher could be filled with so much hatred and want to destroy so many lives.

Aaron approached a group of mourners who stood in a prayer circle. He didn't know them, but two of the people released their hands and allowed him to enter. He looked around and saw Rashad leading the prayer.

"Dear Lord, if it is your will, please heal our community. Allow us the courage to carry on the memory of our brothers and sisters who have passed."

Aaron noticed that although Rashad had his eyes closed, the boy spoke with conviction and passion.

"Lord, we pray that you bless each and every person here who has been harmed by this tragic event." Rashad stopped for a moment. "We have been through a lot." He opened his eyes and wiped a tear away from his face. Looking around to others, he said, "If you have something on your heart, let God hear your voice."

Aaron looked to the ground and spoke, "Dear God, I lost my best friend. I pray that you give her solace and let her find peace. Lord God on High, Victoria cared for people. She cared for the children. Lord, God, please take her into your loving embrace. Please care for her and let your light shine on those passed." He paused for a moment, choking on the emotions.

◆ ◆ ◆

Mei came to the circle, not as a reporter, but as a member of the community. For once, she needed to grieve. Once a gregarious woman, now she was at a loss of words. But eventually they came. As more people joined the circle, she asked, "May I speak?"

Rashad open his eyes. "Yes, Ma'am. All are welcome here. Please say what is in your heart."

"I want to pray for those who have passed. For we are truly sadden." she said. She was about to say, 'I too had a friend.' But it was her friend who had caused this tragedy. She tried to find the words to speak. After a moment, she said, "Lord, give us hope in our sorrow, and allow us to cherish their memory." She paused, "God take all who were killed and give them a new home in Heaven. In Jesus' name, I pray. Amen."

Basil Scion

Biography

Basil Scion was born in 1970 while his mother and father were living in Baltimore, Maryland. His parents moved to the South shortly thereafter. Basil lived in Atlanta until 1989 at which time he left to pursue higher education.

Basil Scion is passionate about sports. Kayaking is his favorite sport, but he does enjoy football and baseball.

As far as education goes, he believes that more emphasis should be placed on creativity today by teachers and that parents also should be more actively involved in the lives of their children.

Outside of sports, he thoroughly enjoys shooting videos of various subjects and creating inspiring graphics. Salvador Dali is his favorite artist and a big inspiration.

www.ingramcontent.com/pod-product-compliance
Lightning Source LLC
Chambersburg PA
CBHW050942120626
46552CB00001B/333